STRANGERS
FROM A STRANGE
WORLD

A SHORT STORY COLLECTION OF MYSTERIES

CHRISTIAN STAHL

STRANGERS

FROM A STRANGE WORLD

A Short Story Collection of Mysteries

Christian Stahl

STRANGERS FROM A STRANGE WORLD

THE EVIL DOUBLE LIFE

THE HAUNTING

THE UNREACHABLE SEA WIFE

CAFÉ LISBON

THE GIRL FROM THE SALVATION ARMY

THE LONDON MARATHON

RESCUE FROM DEVIL'S ISLAND

THE BREACH

THE DISFIGURED PAINTING

Christian Stahl

Details of all the author's available books and upcoming titles

can be found at:

www.shortstoriesforbeginners.com

STRANGERS FROM A STRANGE WORLD

Even now, Ben Iglesias doesn't know what happened that day. The memory came to him in fragments; a cacophony of sound and vision that didn't quite fit together into a coherent picture. It was like sand between his fingers, trickling away every time he tried to reach for it.

He remembered the flight. It should have been a routine trip, from Mars to Earth, a journey that he had planned extensively, a journey he had already taken four times before. For his crew, it had been their first time piloting a ship, but they'd had simulation experience and were well-prepared. Nothing should have gone wrong.

The moment they had entered Earth's orbit, the system went down. A warning light flickered on at the control panel, and then the alarms had started, blasting through the spacecraft with growing intensity. The atmosphere turned dense, and at some point amid the chaos, Ben had lost consciousness.

When he woke up, everything was silent. The alarms had ceased, and only the thin red strobe of the emergency sign punctuated the air above him.

The bodies of his four crewmates were sprawled around him, unmoving. He knew they were dead. Their eyes were still open, staring blankly at the ceiling of the craft, and their chests were still.

The emergency lights were on, but everything else was dead. There was no static, no alarm, no warnings beeping on the console. Just silence.

He couldn't tell how long had passed since the spacecraft had landed. It must have crashed, judging by the state of chaos around him, debris and equipment toppled over. Somewhere in the rear of the craft, he could hear electricity sparking, and the air was tinged with the smell of burning. He had to get out, before the whole thing went up in flames.

Climbing to his feet, he staggered over to the control panel and took in the readings that were displayed on the cracked monitor. None of them made sense. The weather, the coordinates, even the time and date... none of it could be correct. The readings must have gone haywire when the system malfunctioned. He pressed the button on the comms system, trying to reach base, but it was dead. Everything was dead.

When he glanced out of the spacecraft's narrow windows, he struggled to understand what he was seeing. He should have been somewhere on the shore, near La Havana Cuba. They'd come down just over the Caribbean Sea. But instead, the landscape stretched on in shades of yellow and brown.

Ignoring the pain in his head, Ben eventually exited the spacecraft, leaving behind the bodies of his crew, and stepped out onto the white sand. The desert seemed to roll on forever, towards a burning sun that made mirages on the horizon. The atmosphere was stifling, and according to his tech, there was only 60% oxygen present. He could feel his chest tightening up, but forced himself to take slow, calm breaths. Panicking would only make it worse.

Where was he?

All he could see, for miles around, was that glinting golden sea of sand. No buildings or man-made structures, just dunes and peaks and a few rocks in the distance.

He was in the middle of nowhere. The supplies he had on the spaceship were likely trapped beneath the debris, and he didn't know how long he had before the craft went up in flames. He had to get away from it, but where would he go?

There was nowhere *to* go but forward, towards the burning sun. The air here was sweltering and sweat beaded along his brow as he slipped over the sand in his space suit. He'd have to take it off sooner or later, but for now, he'd rather keep it on, if only for the extra layer of protection it afforded.

He kept walking, the sands shifting constantly underfoot as the sun bore down on him, until his body gave in to exhaustion. The crash had already weakened him, and when he glanced back, he realized he'd barely made it more than a few meters away from the ship itself.

Sinking to his knees in the sand, Ben closed his eyes. How had this happened? What had caused the ship's system to fail, bringing them down to Earth hundreds of miles off course? It didn't make sense to him. His crew was dead, and he was all alone. He doubted he would last much longer in this heat anyway, not without food or water. A sense of complete hopelessness descended on him, and he began to shake. Why had this happened to him? What had he done to deserve such a horrible twist of fate?

Wind buffeted the side of his face, blowing sand against his eyelids. He couldn't stay here. He had to keep moving. Even if it hurt, he couldn't just give up.

When his eyes flickered back open, he realized he was not alone. Cresting the peak of a nearby sand dune was a figure.

Ben reached up vigorously to rub his eyes, thinking he was hallucinating, but then more of them appeared, small dark shadows blotting the horizon.

People. There were *people*.

Ben tried to climb to his feet, but his knees buckled again, and he landed hard in the sand.

The first figure began shuffling down the dune towards him, and he stayed where he was. From what he could see, they did not carry weapons, and seemed more curious than aggressive.

They were like no people he had ever seen before, but he didn't know what else they could be. They had the same build and features of humans, but they were also much shorter.

As the group of people reached him, they clustered around him in a semi-circle staring down at him. But even on his knees, Ben was almost as tall as they were standing up.

There were mostly women present, and a couple of men, but their skin was dark and painted with chalk, different to his pale skin and light hair. Their eyes, too, were unusual. Like dark stones, set deep into their faces. One woman in particular caught his eye; her eyes were black and shining, almost like a cat's. She cocked her head slightly when she realised he was looking at her.

Who were these people? Were they Australian Aborigines? There was some resemblance, but they were smaller and thinner, almost skeletal in appearance, and their skin was rough like the sand.

The man in front of him pulled a water skin from the string around his waist and offered it to Ben. When Ben hesitated, he gestured for him to drink, tipping the skin towards him.
Ben finally nodded, taking the water from him with trembling, sand-burned hands. He took a sip, feeling the cold liquid wash down his throat, and then another, careful not to take too much.

"Thank you," he rasped, handing the water back to the man.

The stranger then motioned for Ben to follow. Two of the women came forward to help Ben to his feet, one of them being the woman with the cat-like eyes, who was at least four heads shorter than him. Despite their small bodies, they had surprising strength, and managed to get him to his feet with minimal effort.

The man gestured again for Ben to follow, so he did.

It wasn't like he had anywhere else to go. Only forward.

The mysterious people led him through the desert, over the dunes and peaks, until they came to the valley of stones that Ben had seen in the distance. When he glanced back, his spacecraft was nothing but a smudge on the horizon.

The rocks here were white, sun-bleached, and covered with small holes. The woman with dark eyes tapped the stone with her finger, white chalk smearing onto her skin, and gestured for him to look inside.

He complied, stepping up to a hole that was big enough for him to squeeze through.

Inside was a cave system with a high-arching ceiling, stalactites hanging down like teeth. From deeper inside, he could hear water striking stone. The rocks must soak up moisture and deposit it deep in the system. He looked in amazement at the woman next to him, and her lips curved into a faint smile. Ben found himself smiling back.

Someone shouted behind him, a word he did not recognize, in a language he did not know, and he turned.

The man from before was standing before him, holding out a strange looking fruit. He mimicked eating it, before holding it out to Ben. He took it with a grateful nod, sinking his teeth into the soft flesh. The fruit was like nothing he had tasted before, filling his mouth with a sweet, tangy aroma. With food and water in his stomach, he could feel his strength returning. He was saved, after all. He owed his life to these people. But now more than ever, he realized he was stuck here. These people lived in the desert, lived off the land. They had no infrastructure, no supplies. Just the remnants of a civilization. Surely that meant there was nothing here.

Nowhere to go, no method of travel but to walk across the sands.

He was still alone. He could not speak with these people, did not know their language, their customs. He was a stranger here.

Once he had finished the fruit, licking the juices from his fingers, he tried to thank the people around him. He got to his knees and pressed his head to the dusty rocks, trying to communicate his gratitude for saving him.

A hand gently touched his shoulder, and when he looked up, he was staring into those beautiful black eyes again. The woman shook her head gently, signaling for him to stand, so he did.

"Thank you," he said again, unsure if they could understand him. "My name is *Ben.*" He pointed to himself, repeating his name.

"Ben," the people around him repeated.

The man pointed to himself next and said in a slow voice: "Ruma."

"Ruma," Ben repeated, nodding, then turned to the woman expectantly. She seemed surprised to be asked, but also gestured to herself.

"Lera."

"Lera," he said softly. "Lera."

The woman seemed to grow sheepish, taking a step back, and Ben smiled in amusement. Perhaps they weren't so strange after all.

That night, Ben lay under the stars, cushioned by the rocks in the valley. He could not sleep. His thoughts would not settle, going round and round in his head like a sputtering engine.

What now?

He had been saved by these people, given food and water and shelter, but what came next? His ship was broken, his crew was dead. Nobody knew where he was; nobody would come looking for him. He could hardly even tell how long had passed since he was last at the space station. The journey between Mars and Earth already seemed so long ago. It felt as though time had already changed, propelling him into a future he wasn't expecting. The world here was not the world he remembered, but different. Like he had been away for many more years than he knew.

Perhaps he had. Time could be a fickle thing in space. And the crash, landing amid this unknown land, the coordinates and temperature, everything that had been displayed on the ship's control panel – everything he thought was incorrect – might not be so far-fetched after all. If their entry into the Earth's orbit had torn through time itself, things would begin to make a lot more sense.

But Ben couldn't be sure. He couldn't communicate with these people, couldn't ask them the year or the day, if they even had the same calendar he was familiar with.

There was no point in pondering things he could not know. It would only drive him mad.

Instead, he should focus on the rational dangers ahead of him. Like the fact that he was trapped here, in the golden sands of some unknown land, without any means of getting back home.

The hopelessness of his situation came crashing back down to him, leaving him gasping for air.

He got up, shaking the dust from his clothes, and went to the edge of the stony ridge, looking out across the darkness. The stars shone brighter here than he had ever seen, creating a silver mist along the horizon.

A figure stepped up beside him, silent as a cat.

"Lera," he whispered.

She said something in her tongue, and he looked at her. She was pointing up to the sky. She said it again, and he realized she was telling him the word for the stars. He repeated it, looking up at where he'd come from. He'd come from the stars. A place as mysterious and unknown as this. But a place he had once called home.

"Home," he said out loud, and Lera repeated it in her gentle voice.

"This is your home?" Ben continued, gesturing around him.

Lera squinted, trying to gauge the meaning of his words, before nodding.

She pointed to the rocks, and then the sand, saying each word slowly so that he could repeat it after her.

The night passed like this, the two of them sitting on the rocks while Lera tried to teach him her language.

After a few days, Ben was starting to get the basics. With nowhere else to go, he'd decided to stay. These people had no qualms about taking him in, and they provided him food and water from their stores, and in return, he used his stronger body to help them shift rocks and collect water from inside the caves.

A week passed, and then another.

Ben began to change. He grew accustomed to a life among the rocks and the sand. His skin began to turn golden, taking on the same rough, sandy texture as the sand dwellers. He grew more confident in their language, achieving basic communication, thanks to Lera's instruction.

There were still moments where, in the silence and the solitude, he'd feel a sense of displacement, like he didn't really belong here. And the memories of the crash, the mystery of what had happened, still haunted him. He would have nightmares of what happened, waking up in the dead of night in a panic, mourning his dead crew, his vulnerability.

But then Lera would be there, soothing him with her gentle voice, stroking her delicate fingers through his hair.

He grew closer to her over those weeks, almost never straying from her side. They collected water together, travelled across the sands together, to the only trees that bore fruit for miles around. She was the community's healer too, and she taught him how to make medicines from the plants that grew there, crushing them into pastes that healed the sores and scrapes they sustained from living in such a harsh environment.

He began to forget his past, who he used to be. He forgot what it was like to travel among the stars, ferrying his ship from one planet to the other. He remembered what it was like to live *beneath* the stars, to feel small and insignificant under a vast sky. The mystery of what happened that day faded with dawn.

His nightmares faded. He was no longer plagued by the desire to know the truth, to know what had happened to his spacecraft and his crew, to know why his ship had crashed without reason. It didn't matter anymore. That part of his life was over now, buried in the sand.

This was his new life, here in this strange new world, with these strange new people.

He had a home here, a new calling, and a woman who he had begun to love.

The troubles of his past did not bother him here. So here he would stay.

THE EVIL DOUBLE LIFE

He didn't know whether it was the strangest situation in his life, or something new, a kind of unknown power that had met him for the first time. He was about to draw a pistol when a ray of light appeared, and a bright translucent arm stretched out towards him with an open hand. Someone wanted to help him — darkness and light. And then the monotonous, shrill sound of the alarm clock ripping him from his sleep. What a strange dream. It was now five-thirty in the morning. Still sleepy, he groped with his left hand for the device to turn off the ringing.

Slowly he pulled himself together. What a shitty day today. He rubbed his eyes, yawned, and ran his fingers through his short, tousled hair.

His pajamas were wrinkled, and Oliver was a little annoyed to have been torn so brutally from his beautiful dream. He had already forgotten what he had dreamed about, but he had no doubt that it had been beautiful. When he fell back on his pillow, he noticed saliva dribbling from his mouth, whereupon he threw the pillow to the foot of the bed in disgust.

"Honey, what time is it? Do you always have to leave so early?" groaned a drowsy voice coming from the indefinable pile of long, dark hair and blanket lying next to him.

"You know how that works," he said, trying to sound reasonably cheerful. Always think positively, Elisabeth used to say, and that's exactly what he was going to do this morning. It would probably be hard, but you didn't have to let it show right away.

Oliver got out of bed quietly, slipped into his slippers and headed for the bathroom, careful to be as silent as possible so his wife could continue sleeping.

The water was cold. Pretty cold, but it was just what he needed. "Start the day in a good mood, then you'll do your job even better," he murmured to himself.

After he had shaved and applied deodorant, and aftershave, he also felt much fresher. While brushing his teeth, he crept into the bedroom as quietly as possible and put on his silver Rolex, which he had placed on the bedside table the night before. When he had finished, he went to the training and dressing room.

The room was about twenty square meters and was dominated by an elongated, externally mirrored cabinet, which was juxtaposed with various exercise machines — an exercise bike, a treadmill and various weight-lifting options.

Oliver worked out regularly in the evenings, so all he needed in the mornings, were fifty push-ups and an equal number of sit-ups to get his circulation going without breaking out in a sweat.

Oliver drank his morning coffee black and without sugar, but in return, he enjoyed plenty of orange juice and vitamin-enriched energy drinks as a counterbalance. While he had toast, first with peanut butter and then with orange marmalade, he casually scrolled through his cell phone—nothing important apparently, which confirmed his thoughts. In fact, he wasn't really interested in it, but he made sure to answer all messages briefly. The Eagles boomed from the speakers of his three-thousand-dollar Bose stereo system.

Oliver preferred Armani. He put on the crisp white shirt, slipped into his elegant, tailor-made anthracite suit and tied the tie knot. He then grabbed the business bag, which he had already packed the night before, and prepared to leave his house discreetly—a last look in the mirror. Perfect. 6:20. The metro was, of course, delayed, as it was every day. But Oliver had already taken that into account. As usual, it wasn't very full, but it would fill up along the thirty-minute ride, and by the time he finally got off, it would become quite cramped. He reached his destination, the central station, not a moment too early. Oliver, like most people, didn't really feel comfortable in large crowds, but he didn't have too much of a problem with that either. The more people stayed in one place, the less he attracted attention in the crowd. He liked that.

Oliver wore a black trench coat, so he was spared unpleasant questions about his clothes and appearance.

It was now 6:45 am, and he got out to get back into another carriage. The fat black woman opposite him had been staring for too long. He decided never to ride in the first carriage again. Oliver wondered if he should try something now and then, do something stupid. It would be fun to count to three and punch the old auntie in the brain.

Oliver's head shake was barely noticeable. *Not today*, he thought. But, he hoped there weren't any more deviant creatures like that old bag or even migrants. Still, the old aunt had had such a strange look, who was she? The important thing was that she finally looked away.

Exactly twenty minutes later he got off at the central station.

Then he only had to walk two blocks further to reach his

destination. Wharton Business Building.

Oliver greeted the doorman with a subtle nod, and marched

purposefully toward the elevator, picking up his pace just

before he entered the company's open-glass door.

"Hey Porter, how are you doing this morning?"

Oliver turned. Right behind the door was O'Neill, the old

bastard. Oliver nodded at the fat middle-aged man and tried

something similar, a polite smile. O'Neill was an unpleasant

colleague whom he usually ignored.

"Still on Junior's Account?" asked O'Neill, whose

weather-beaten skin looked as if it would completely rot off in

ten years at the latest. Oliver had to control himself not to

make a disgusted face.

"Oh... of course," he replied and put on a playful grin that

was meant to express satisfaction and a little bragging.

Feelings that he actually didn't have. He just didn't care about

it at the moment.

"Wow, then you must really be the lucky one," said

O'Neill with a laugh and patted Oliver on the shoulder.

It was supposed to represent something like cordiality, Oliver thought and chewed at his jaw, although he had nothing in his mouth.

In the long hallway, the two men were met by a young, attractive woman in a cream-colored trouser suit, probably Yves Saint Lauren. Maybe twenty-eight. *Definitely a fucking fuckable* thing, Oliver mused. He caught himself looking at her and noticed, slightly amused, O'Neill staring at her bottom. *Old, ugly fuck, forget it. Just forget it. If anything, that's mine, one way or another.*

They reached the company's reception hall. Luckily, O'Neill would turn left here. That saved him at least some of the stupid, petty chatter that would undoubtedly still await him.

But no, this couldn't be true, today fat O'Neill followed him.

"I heard Cherry and Todd got caught doing something," offered O'Neill.

The chatter was now almost pre-programmed. The man was just rewinding a voice recorder that some crazy surgeon had transplanted behind his vocal cords.

"Did you know they were involved? I'm not a big fan of this woman's talk," he chuckled, "but it's worth a few words about it."

In another ten yards or five seconds, he would reach his office.

"That's it," Oliver said. "It was nice talking to you... uh... O'Neill, right?"

O'Neill winked at him and snapped his finger in a playful gesture. *What a jerk.*

No sooner had Oliver taken a seat behind his screen when he saw a dark figure coming towards him from the corner of his eye.

"Ah, Mister Porter. Good to see you," a sonorous female voice called out to him. It was Elli Marples. She worked in an office two corridors away and was a Jones, Meyer and Champs employee, a second-rate law firm in Oliver's opinion, but with a first-class reputation — at least if you believed Elli. Since he had begun working here, the old smoker, who was in her late forties, always greeted him in an over-friendly way.

"You're looking sharp, Olli. May I call you Olli?" She dropped her eyes with a hint of embarrassment. "In the meantime, we can get to know each other a little."

"Of course," Oliver replied with a suppressed smile.

But he knew immediately that this worn-out frigate was flirting with him for business reasons only. Oliver had long since given up having any illusions about people, especially women, although he trusted his wife, so far.

The day went by meaninglessly, phone calls, letters, accountant crap. But he stayed focused, nothing upset him, he was quite proud about that. And still, one day less. Oliver was on his way home, not far from the metro. He walked nervously through a pedestrian tunnel and finally arrived at the somewhat run-down apartment building where he had rented a small apartment. Nobody seemed to be there except the caretaker, who was probably repairing something somewhere in the basement.

"Hey mister," shouted a voice, greeting him, when Oliver was on the stairs between the second and the third floor. The caretaker had an oriental accent. He was probably an Indian or a Pakistani.

"Good evening," Oliver returned dryly.

"Please do not enter the basement. There has been a small mishap down here. Please excuse me."

"No problem." Oliver now looked down the hallway through the railing so he could see the man below. He smiled affirmatively.

He continued up the hallway until he finally arrived at a door. It was quite a simple door, but sturdy and soundproof. Oliver had installed it himself. An exact replica of the original.

There was a peephole at eye level through which people standing in the corridor could be observed. He unlocked the door and entered the small apartment. Opposite the entrance was a window darkened by a roller shutter. In front of it was a desk with a laptop sitting on it. Oliver turned the computer on.

The room was sparsely furnished. The table. A revolving chair. Two high, angular cupboards. Oliver opened one of them and grabbed a revolver from the top shelf. Sitting in his chair, he playfully spun the drum.
He opened the drawer under the tabletop. Inside were several disposable cell phones — without a contract. He turned one on and checked a few of the numbers stored in it. At the same time, he typed something into the computer. Shortly afterwards he closed the program, and for a fraction of a

second, the desktop showed the picture of a young, well-dressed gentleman.

Oliver put on a headset and turned on another program. *Let's see if one of my middlemen has a new assignment for me.*

While he was waiting for the software to load, he dug out a packet of bullets and played with them, slipping them one by one between his fingers. He glanced into the next room. The door was open. Only the reddish glow of small high-tech devices could be seen — otherwise, the room was dark. It was precisely three minutes past eight.

At that exact same time, Elisabeth was sitting on her white couch with a glass of red wine. She was scanning through a magazine on the wide-screen plasma TV on the topic, *Sleep Disorders — A sign of a disturbed relationship with the employer?* And was about to fall asleep.

Of course, she could not relate to the subject matter of the program. At least not really. She had never worked before. She had married Oliver right after university. She had actually grown up in a strict Catholic home although she didn't believe in conservative, bourgeois role relationships. Then again, it was her husband who brought the money home. He earned really well, but he worked such terribly long hours, at least that's what she thought.

Quite often, Oliver would come home very late. And this was one of those days. She waited impatiently, wanting nothing more than to be taken in his arms. It had been such a disaster for her... She sighed and closed her eyes briefly.

Suddenly a small red dot appeared in the darkness from her bedroom window. After a few seconds, the dot multiplied to many dots, which slowly came closer. Had she paid closer attention, she would certainly have heard a soft rustling from outside, but Elisabeth was completely lost in thought. Her glass was empty, and she stood up, striding towards the kitchen, to pour herself another one.

Finally, she heard the familiar turning of the key in the door. Olli. At last. She smelled his perfume, yes, it was him. The hallway light came on. She saw his shadow on the floor.

"Honey? Where were you? I had a terribly long day," she said, moaning exaggeratedly.

Silence. A moment passed.

"Honey?"

A short moment of silence, then she stuck her head out of the half-opened door.

It was her husband. He was pale.

"Olli, What happened?"

"Nothing. I believe nothing. I was just thinking...I might have heard something."

"My love," Elisabeth said. Ignoring Oliver's words of concern.

At that very moment, a loud clicking sound was heard. Glass shattered and with a loud bang, the door opened behind them. Many men in black erupted into the house.

Oliver didn't know what to do. He reached into the inside pocket of his long, dark coat and pulled out something silvery. But before he could react, there was a soft click and a bullet drilled into his head. He collapsed lifelessly to the floor. A second of silence followed the thud of his fall. Then Elisabeth started to scream. She screamed as loud and as long as she could. Strange looking silhouettes appeared just before she dropped to her knees out of shock and despair. She recognized the letters SWAT printed in white on the dark creatures that had stormed into the room.

Later on, just before midnight, Elizabeth was huddled up on a couch somewhere, wrapped in a warm blanket. Next to her sat a police psychologist and a doctor who had given her a Valium. She had suffered a terrible shock.

The silver object that Oliver had tried to pull out of his coat had been a cell phone, not a gun. She realized they had shot the wrong man, her husband.

The only gun he had was a 38 caliber revolver legally registered in his name. They must have broken into the wrong house. The mistake was unforgivable, and the officer in charge would probably be suspended for the time being. Next door to the Porters lived a man named Sammy Smith. A professional killer, who under the name 'tin man' had been carrying out assassinations for the Mafia and their employers for years.

However, in Oliver's coat pocket, a memory stitch with a video in it was recovered. As it turned out, he earned most of his income by shooting and distributing gay porn with a tragic-comic plot. Not as a successful accountant, as his wife had always believed.

The frame on the videotape which the district attorney Schmidt used to narrate the fatal events and strange double life to his colleagues, revealed naked men on a large bed in a cramped room. In the background, a half-open door was visible. It led to another sparsely furnished room where one could just make out a few angular cupboards, a table on which

a laptop was placed, in front of a rotating chair.

Only years later, Elisabeth found out that her husband had

been trying to change his job, possibly his life, years before

the accident. From old documents, letters and emails, she

could tell that he had visited a priest only one day before his

death. When she found out, Elizabeth got down on her knees

and cried.

If he had tried earlier, everything would have been

different, flashed through her mind.

This was all a year ago. Now, Elizabeth led a quasi-new

life, had even found a new partner, and her job satisfied her

more. It was the darkness of that time that helped her find new

ways. She remembered her depression had become so strong

that she had had a spiritual experience. Since then, her life had

become better, although only very slowly. Not perfect, but

with spiritual progression.

THE HAUNTING

The grass is still damp from the overnight rain, even now in the late morning when Mari and a few others walk slowly from the common room of the nursing home towards the pavilion. A nurse guides the small group, not one of them younger than ninety.

"Mari, maybe you'd like to share with everyone the story you told me yesterday,' says the nurse, George, as she arranges the chairs.

Mari nods. "Yes. I was thinking about it last night. There were things I forgot to tell you. Terrible things. Things I thought that I would never forget.'

"Don't scare everyone, now,' says George, smiling.

"This happened when I was very young,' Mari began. An old man walks towards them, older even than any of the people sitting in the pavilion. Hunched over with age, he almost resembles a gargoyle from a cathedral spire. George pauses, offering to help, but the old man waves her away and takes a seat with the rest of the group and swivels his pale, watery blue eyes towards Mari.

"Are you new here?' one of them asks.

The old man seems to nod.

"You're so familiar,' says Mari. "But I can't remember
from where, I'm sorry. Maybe I'm forgetting faces now.'

"Tell us the story, Mari,' says one of the old men. "George
says it's a good one.'

Mari nods, but her eyes don't leave the face of the stranger.
"As I was saying, this all happened a very long time ago.'

"I was on holiday, in Genoa. Bill and I had just got engaged. We
didn't see much of the city. We were so happy just being together
that it was enough to walk along the shore. I didn't care that we
were missing out on seeing the Palazzi dei Rolli.

It became our habit to go down to the harbor and watch the
sunrise, listen to the gulls and all the fishermen starting work.
This morning we walked farther than usual, around to the dry
docks, where the ships are repaired and built. There was one ship
in particular that caught our attention. It was a new ocean liner,
quite small. It was designed to take fewer passengers, but it
would offer a luxury service. The design was cutting edge for the
time, in particular its double-skinned hull.

I remember seeing it half-complete, hanging out of the
water. Like a skeleton. There were two workmen arguing on

shore. They seemed very upset. But of course they were speaking in Italian – I couldn't understand them.

Bill and I got married that summer. We didn't have any ideas about our honeymoon, but one morning Bill opened the newspaper and there was an advertisement for the ship. Its maiden voyage, from Southampton to New York. It seemed perfect.

It was extraordinary to see the boat completed. It spanned three decks, and where most cruise ships of the time were bulky, like a tall building turned on its side, this ship was sleek, almost like a superyacht, except no one had built one of them before. It was the first of its kind. It balanced on the water like a knife, and its black hull gleamed like polished marble.

Those first nights – I don't think I've ever danced so much! The band played late into the night and most of us on board were young and there to enjoy ourselves. But there was one man who wasn't having fun. He wouldn't dance, he only sat there in the corner, drinking. He was a crooked, sour-faced man. He had dark circles under his blue eyes, like he hadn't slept in weeks. His clothes were expensive, but unclean. I remember thinking he must have been a manual worker, because his hands were covered in tiny white scars. Everyone thought it best to keep away from him, but I made the mistake of talking to him one night. He claimed to have been an engineer who worked on the construction of the ship and he told me this nasty little story about punishing a worker who'd made mistakes during the ship's construction. I could smell the alcohol on his breath, so I didn't take him seriously. It just seemed like the ravings of an unpleasant drunk.

The thing is, I think part of the reason we all danced so late is that none of us wanted to go to bed. Because as soon as you went to bed all you could listen to were the sounds of the ship at night. The wind and the waves and the creaking of the hull. These were all normal sounds, but there were other things. Voices. At first I thought it must be my mind playing tricks on me, but when I finally told Bill what I heard, he said that he had heard it too. A friend we had made on board, Lucy, said maybe it was a ghost. People were much more superstitious back then, it didn't seem like a strange thing to think.

But then every night we'd get dressed up and we'd go to the ballroom, where the musicians were waiting for us in their evening suits. And the music would start and we'd get to our feet and dance and dance and forget all about the voices.

I can still remember the feeling of being out in the Atlantic, so far from everything. Nothing but the ocean for miles, dark clouds rolling across the endless sky, the gentle pitching of the ship whenever we met a wave.

A week into the voyage, the strange voices became harder to ignore. We could tell the crew members were edgy – they were hearing the voices as well. And not just voices. There were knocking sounds all over the ship, in different places every night. Like something was trying to claw through the walls.

Every night we'd keep going up to the ballroom, but no one danced anymore. Our friend Lucy whispered to us that she was cancelling her return ticket. She wasn't alone. The only person who didn't seem upset was the drunkard engineer. He sat at the bar every night, drinking and laughing to himself. We thought about cancelling our ticket, but we were a young married couple; we didn't have much money. Our return ticket was our only way home.

The night before we arrived in New York we heard screaming. It was clear, but distant. As if you could hear someone screaming from just over there, inside the nursing home. The moment we landed there was nearly a stampede to get off the ship.

We only spent a few days in New York. It wasn't as long as we'd hoped, but Bill had to get back to work. The city must be so different today, but even then it was an extraordinary place. I'd never seen so many people all at once. And the skyscrapers!

It was almost enough to make us forget about how strange our journey had been. By the time we were getting back on board the ship, we were feeling like maybe somehow we had imagined the whole thing.

That first night, the ballroom was nearly empty. Even some of the musicians had decided not to come back on the return voyage, and those that were left played to drown out the screaming. On the third night, we were woken, the noise was like a loud, dull thud, different to anything we had heard so far. Bill ran out of the cabin. When he finally came back, he was pale as a sheet. "Don't go out there," he said. "A boiler exploded. There were six men in the room. They're all dead."

.I went looking for the drunkard who'd haunted the bar on our outward voyage. He had claimed to be an engineer working on the ship, so I wondered if he knew something about the boiler. I couldn't find him. I guessed he must have stayed on shore in New York.

The closer we got to home, the fainter the screaming sounds became, until by the time we were disembarking at Southampton we could hardly hear them at all. They weren't even like screams anymore. Just a faint, desperate whine.

I kept hearing stories about that ship as the years went by. Accidents, people jumping overboard for no reason. People said that it was cursed. One day, Bill looked up from reading the newspaper and told me the ship was gone. It had been coming into port in Hamburg it hit an old mine, and sunk. No one died, thankfully. Still, I was sad. Even though that trip had been the strangest month of my life, it was my honeymoon. That beautiful, state-of-the-art ship. Gone.

Only that wasn't the end of it. When they dragged it up from the sea floor and dismantled it, when they peeled back the double-skinned hull, they found two bodies. Skeletons. Trapped between the outer and the inner hull. And sure enough, two riveters had disappeared during the construction of the ship all those years ago in Genoa. Finally, they had been found.'

Mari breaks off. The group turns towards the stranger who had joined them. He's laughing.

"I'm sorry,' he says. "I'm sorry to laugh, it's just…'

Laughter shakes his ancient frame. His hands wipe away tears of mirth.

"I do know you from somewhere,' says Mari.

"It was a long time ago. I drink less, now. Back then I drank to drown out their screams but now… now you see all I can do is laugh. I remember you from the ballroom. The honeymooners.' The old man leans forward in his seat. "Do you know how perfectly my designs needed to be executed for that ship to succeed? And all the time I was surrounded by lazy scroungers who refused to pull their weight. Those two were the worst of the lot. It was easy to lure them into the space between the hulls. "Last minute welding," I said. "I'll pay you double." They believed it. Well, it was true in a way. As soon as they were inside I had the hatch welded shut.'

The crowd of old people murmur in discomfort. "Get away from us,' says one woman. "You're cursed, like that ship.'

Mari sits very still, an expression of horrified revulsion on her face. The old man shrugs. "I'm too old for jail,' he says. "And I already know hell.'

He lifts his black hat in farewell. They watch him walk away across the damp grass. George, the nurse, watches him anxiously. Without warning, the old man lifts his face to the overcast sky, and screams.

"The same sound,' Mari whispers to herself. "The same voice.'

THE UNREACHABLE SEA WIFE

The whispers of the waves crept in through the netted curtains that covered the balcony doors that I've left open. The Spanish sea breeze still feels foreign and peculiar to me; I suppose it's a reminder that I'm not where I'm supposed to be. The morning air I'm used to is full of fumes of foods being prepared for the Asian markets, I miss that warm, comforting smell. Even when you could hear market traders shouting to one another, their tone came across as friendly. Home seems further away than ever now that I know I can't get there. And so does she. Our regular messages make things better temporarily, but once the day has gone, the bed feels empty and no message can fill that.

The little money I have doesn't feel worth saving. There's barely enough to cover the costs of transport to the nearest airport, so why bother even considering scraping together funds for a flight that costs nearly as much as a house deposit? Every time I come close to beginning to save up, I find myself back in the pub; repeating my ordeal to any regular who's willing to listen again. Before long, I notice how my words seem to dribble out and my voice is just a whir of noise that I can't properly concentrate on. When the football begins, anyone who was listening stops, apart from the occasional remark or frown when I accidentally criticize the wrong team or player.

Then the routine continues. I wake up to the churning of the ceiling fan, barely creating a single waft of air in the sticky, humid bedroom. The heat is usually what wakes me up, and that's how I know it's most likely early afternoon. That's how I know I've wasted yet another day. I often find myself pondering over how my life has come to this, "So much life ahead of you, Tim" my grandma would always say, and I feel ashamed at the thought of her seeing me now. I then contemplate where my life will go from here. Sometimes it feels like I'm completely trapped and that one day someone will find me dead in this very bed, I'll be Tim- the drunk from the football bars who drank himself to death. I don't think I'm awake when I have these thoughts, because sometimes the scenes are too vivid to have been created by my imagination alone. There's flies nibbling at my lifeless body as it rots—waiting for someone to come and find me. I wake up panting, relieved to be alive and then disappointed by having no need to wake up.

Other times as I drift in between a deep sleep and being conscious of my sore, hungover body and the accumulating damage I'm doing to it. The sound of the Spanish shore influences my mind and I dream of being rocked in a sailing boat.

I remember my lifelong dream of being an owner of something, a house or anything that really belongs to me, and now it is obvious that there is such a thing, a manageable sailboat they can sail off into the sunset to find my unreachable future wife who for that matter also belongs to me. And If I ever do a solo sailing half around the world I will call my boat *Sea Wife.*

I can hear the mast of the boat squeaking and the sails flapping as the wind carries me along the waves. I'm lying with my back flat against the deck, looking at the clouds as they tumble and twirl through the sky. The rhythmic swaying of the ship soothes me; it's almost as comforting as the thought of the boat taking me away. Away from Spain and my spiral into some sort of catastrophe and maybe towards Asia. It continues to rock me until my mind has completely left the bedroom and the whirring ceiling fan, a deep sleep begins that I don't want to wake up from.

Eventually I do wake up. Five hours I guess is how long I've slept for, there's another message from her that I don't remember seeing. She's not even asking when I'll be back now, but if. I can't respond because I don't know the answer. I wish I did. Things would be more bearable if I at least knew how much longer I'd have to endure this. I feel like I've lost my true self here, like I left myself behind when I left Asia. It's not the same as when I left Britain for Asia; the rural areas that were coated in a rich green colour, blossom and tranquil waters combined with the cities that were packed with people and possibilities felt like my natural habitat. Whilst a part of me will always belong to Britain, another part will always long for Asia, anyways, I am still stuck here in Spain.

I sit up in my bed, the sheets crumpled in a pile by my feet. A fly swirls in from the balcony and heads towards me. He inspects me and then leaves. Perhaps he's checking to see if I'm a rotting dead body yet, like the one I become in my dreams. I start to realise that will become a reality if I don't do something now. Initially, my mind is full of useless ideas, so I open up my laptop and begin looking for answers. A couple of YouTube videos enforce what I am already starting to understand—I need to change things now. I check the costs of flights once more, but the prices have only gone up if anything. Some suggestions appear for taking a few ferries, however there's no direct route so it would end up costing me as much as the plane tickets. As I start tracing the different courses the ferries and cargo ships would take, I remember my dream about the boat.

Whilst I'm no expert in sailing, I don't remember it as being particularly challenging from what I can recall of the day my mother and I hired a boat when I was younger. That could be it, I could sail back to Asia! The trouble is I'd need a boat. I suppose I could hire one and then not return–but they would know who had taken it, it would be a risky move. I head out onto the small balcony where I can stare at the waves rolling in and the horizon: a place I could be crossing sometime soon. My eyes begin to wander to the ground and as they do, I notice what appears to be a headsail propped up against the fence in my neighbour's front garden.

I see a sailboat on a trailer that apparently had been rerigged, repainted and has the motor mounted on the winch post for transport.

Then things begin to come back to me. I remember having a brief conversation with him a few weeks back and he'd mentioned that he was going out to sea for the weekend. I hadn't properly understood what he meant by that until now. In fact, I hadn't understood a lot of what he said; he's German and his English is very limited. I would have perhaps taken a little more time to interpret what he was telling me, but he spoke mostly about himself in a very proud manner and it only made me feel more ashamed of my situation.

I spend the next few days taking my time leaving the apartment to run unimportant errands; the real goal of each trip out is to inspect my neighbor's boat. It's a reasonable size and sits on a trailer that I'm sure I'm capable of pulling. Fortunately, the lane my apartment resides on is quiet and goes directly to the port; the journey to it would be a struggle but, at least it would be short. I don't pay as many visits to the pub, although sometimes I find myself back in there, numbing the harsh reality that, whilst I now have an opportunity to get out of here, the journey ahead isn't going to be easy. Some days it feels easier to back out and stay here for a while. But I've spent time looking at maps, planning out a route and, with any luck, I could be out of here by Christmas and in Asia at some point in the New Year.

The boat is a humble size, a beautiful white 26 footer with a long fin keel and what looked like an unusual large cockpit, certainly a German design probably built for the Baltic Sea; I can feel the excitement and curiosity in my body as I know it's only me who would be using it. The sails are a rich, white fabric; they look as though they've not been out to sea yet. On one evening I get close enough to spot that the boat is called Helga, the dude's dead wife I think.

I stumble back into my apartment. Occasionally I'll pay attention to my reflection in the mirror. The heavy bags under my brown eyes have started to fade, but they'll never completely vanish–like a deep scar. My dark, short hair is still receding more rapidly than I'd like and my thin, bony frame that carries a round tummy caused by beer seems to have plumped up a little. When I bother to shave off the stubble on my chin, my skin appears paler than I remember, although if I spend enough time in the sun, I collect freckles that warm it up.

I then start to pack up my things. I haven't got much to take, just a couple of bags altogether. I look around my nearly empty apartment and realize I have no emotional connection to it–at least none that are positive. I've been here for a while now but almost everyday I hope it'll be my last; that I'll somehow be whisked back to Asia by the next morning. Now, that seems like less of a dream.

Eventually the day I've planned to leave on arrives. I wait until the sky has become dark enough to cover the crime I am about to commit, and I sit listening for movement from my neighbor through the walls although I have a hunch he is not at home. The prospect of what is ahead of me is difficult to comprehend. As I begin to consider the problems that could arise, such as being caught by my neighbor, getting lost at sea, capsizing. I check my phone for messages; it's been a while since I last heard from my girlfriend, once I get back to Asia, I'll look for her. I find that my fingertips are pulsating, and my hands are trembling. I take out the cheap bottle of liquor I had left in the kitchen and begin to swig from it, at first to calm the physical shaking and then to stop my thoughts from persuading me to not go ahead with my endeavors. Perhaps I drink a little too much as I notice the walls around me begin to spin, under my breath, I tell myself to get a grip.

After about half an hour of no noise from the neighbor, it's time for me to begin my journey. The liquor sits at the top of my stomach, but I know this is because I'm nervous. I contemplate sitting for another fifteen minutes, listening out for anything other than silence and then I talk myself out of it; I could sit here all night, building up the courage to leave.

With my bag slumped over my shoulder, I lock up the apartment for the final time. The air feels particularly still tonight, barely any breeze and the only thing I can hear is the occasional insect of some kind chirping in the bushes. I try to tread as lightly as I approach my neighbor's garden, the liquor causes me to sway more than I'd like. The moonlight reflects off of the white hull of the sailing boat. I inspect the windows that overlook the garden; it seems to be lifeless for now. I drop my bags into the boat and release the handbrake of the trailer slowly, the creaking of it interrupts the silence of the night and I wince, looking up at the windows again.

My old but fat-ass pick up truck will do the job to tow it down the road to the docks which I think is about an hour drive. I work as quick as I can to set up a line from the back of the towing boat to the front of the towed boat, trying what is supposed to be a stern tow. That German idiot will be surprised so badly and his face would be worth watching when he finds out his baby is gone.

The journey to the port is much longer than I expected, I'd thought that the lane was relatively downhill but there was a lot more heaving of the trailer and negotiating corners compared to what I had anticipated. I don't remember ever having to do such strenuous physical activity, but there's a survival instinct within me now that urges me to carry on. By the time I arrive at the port, morning has broken, and a few people have started their day near the dock. I am relieved to discover that no one seems to be confused or interested in my behaviour, despite, in my opinion, it being quite bizarre. I take a long rest by the port, facing the sea. For the first time, I pay attention to just how vast it is. If I were to go missing, no one would ever find me.

I let the day creep away as I sip on a bottle of water I have packed, I feel completely sober by now and the magnitude of what I have already done catches up with me, if my neighbor finds me here, how will I explain myself? The thought of that motivates me to continue with my journey, I get up and start tugging the trailer down the shore ramp. Without the alcohol in my system, the work seems even more difficult. I notice sweat trickling down my forehead almost instantly and the skin on my hands is raw from all of the tugging.

My boat is a pig to get off the trailer but with the help of a non-English speaking Spaniard, I finally got the boat into the water and climb in.

The six-horsepower Johnson outboard starts on the first pull and I smuggle the boat out of the marina. I am able to work out the direction of the wind and trim the sails, the lift perhaps could be better, but I keep reefing the mainsail until I am satisfied with my speed. I am hardly out of the port, but between yanking lines and checking the instruments, I look at the sea. Especially now in the morning hours it seems to be more mesmerizing than it was in my dreams, I watch the waves coil up and engulf one another, they make a sloshing noise as they do.

As I get further out to the Mediterranean Sea the waters begin to get choppier. By mid day the wind freshens into the south and *Sea Wife's* heavy bows are chopping with a perceptible shudder into each new wave. Each of the waves seem to be bigger and more violent than the last and, as the boat just about manages to recover from the impact from the last, I wonder whether the next wave will be the one to capsize me. Every one smacks into the boat, almost knocking me off my feet and I get sprayed by the salty seawater until I'm completely soaked. I can't pinpoint the exact moment, but the waters eventually begin to calm.

I further shorten the headsail to reduce the strain on the helm, and once I have recovered from the choppy waters and adjusted my sails again, I put *Sea Wife* on autopilot. Over the next few days, I sleep and rest only disturbed by the radar alarm which I ignore. On the fourth day I spot land in the distance. As I begin to approach it, I grow more certain that my directions and predictions are correct: it's Sardinia. I waste no time in collecting supplies from the local shops and then I sit and reflect on how far away my little Spanish apartment seems now. For the first time, I'm not thinking about the distance I have left to travel, although it is in the back of my mind, I'm proud and excited by the fact that I have managed to negotiate a sailing boat all the way to Sardinia. I have a new energy within me and I'm ready for the adventures, and perhaps risks, that are ahead of me.

The sailing techniques come more naturally to me as I leave Sardinia for Malta. I find myself rhythmically tugging at lines and I seem to have found more of a flow to the routine and I make less clumsy mistakes. The journey over to Malta in general feels smoother than my initial trip and I begin to enjoy sailing, my anxieties over things that could go wrong have settled. I look through my binoculars at some land that I hope is Malta, just in front of it is a small boat, which initially excites me; so far I have only seen the occasional ferry or tanker in the distance and the prospect of seeing people out at sea excites me.

Eventually I am close enough to make out individual figures within the boat. There seems to be several men, I believe, tightly packed into what can't be more than a dinghy. I then realize I may be getting too close to them to avoid a crash. I'm not sure which boat could take responsibility, but we narrowly avoid each other. A concern grows within me that they might attempt to hijack my sailing boat; it's much more substantial than theirs. "Don't you dare come near me," I shout to them. They begin to respond in a language I don't understand, some shouting whilst some seem to be pleading. "I have nothing for you, I have my own troubles to deal with and I don't want you scumbags getting in the way." They start to raise their arms and flap them around in the air, annunciating whatever point they're trying to make. I become aware of the fact that they completely outnumber me, aside from a glass bottle that I could potentially smash, I have very little in the way of defending myself. Even though I am not entirely sure they have understood me, I can tell I have angered them, and I decide to continue to sail towards the island in order to avoid any unnecessary conflict. We exchange looks of disgust as we pass each other and then drift in separate directions.

After a night's sleep that was surprisingly one of the best I've had in a long time, I set off for my next destination: Crete. The temperature slowly creeps up during the day and I find myself struggling to function at my normal pace, everything seems to require a little more effort under the intense heat of the sun. The water is exceptionally clear as I sail closer to the shore. The sea floor looks to be only inches away, and I have to resist the temptation to reach in and take a shell or some seaweed. I'm concerned about dehydrating and overheating if I sleep anywhere that is particularly exposed to the sun. I take my time inspecting several locations before settling on a cool, damp cave. The moisture within the cave drips often throughout the night and each time it wakes me up–I think once I'm sleeping I feel particularly vulnerable; what if my German neighbor has somehow tracked me and his boat down, or what if the migrants have decided to come back ready to return the insult? These thoughts become more rational the darker it gets.

My voyage to Egypt runs smoothly to begin with. I have adjusted to the heat relatively quickly and find it easier to negotiate with the wind this time. Once I approach Egypt, however, things suddenly become complicated. I reach the Suez canal passage and several armed officers greet me in a small ship. Without my permission, they clamber on board my boat. Initially, they say very few words, only looking me up and down and muttering amongst themselves. It makes me wonder what exactly they're after and I notice my t-shirt is drenched in sweat and in general, my appearance has become quite scruffy. I worry about them realizing the boat is stolen; I suppose I can tell them I am my German neighbor if it comes to that.

Two of them stand watching me, they don't have to forcibly stop me, but I'm reluctant to stop the other two who begin digging around in my belongings. "Valuables?" One asks. I don't need to lie; I have nothing sentimental and I've never been particularly materialistic.

"N-no." I respond, blushing as I struggle to get my words out. One of the guards staring at me then begins to tug at my clothes—I think he's after my money. Whilst I'd been sensible and distributed my money into several smaller stashes around the boat, it's inevitable that they will find some of them. He plucks out the wad of notes I have in my back pocket and then another man retrieves some from the tin I'd tucked away. Eventually, I'm pretty sure they've found every penny I own.

"500 dollar." One of the guards shouts at me. That's almost half of what I've got altogether.

"Please no, what can I give you, something else please?"

"500 dollar. That's what we want." I look around frantically for anything of value; money is essential to me at the moment.

"Fine, 550." The guard demands impatiently.

"No! Okay 500, I'll pay 500." I say, defeated. I am far too intimidated by the clunky guns they carry around that I'm sure could kill me without them even needing to pull the trigger. I watch them tuck the notes into their pockets and then toss the rest onto the pile of my belongings they have rummaged through. I look at it pathetically. How is that supposed to get me to Asia? I was already tight for money and now I have no idea how I'm supposed to stretch half of my money to last me for the rest of my journey.

After recovering from my trauma of the canal and the authorities, I reach the Red Sea. I chuckled to myself as I thought of the days when I was naïve enough to believe it was actually red in color. Then I think about my other naiveties; believing I could sail all the way to Asia without any issues was one. I look down at the churning water; it's very dark, much richer and opaque than any sea I'd seen before. Nothing like the clarity of the water in Crete. The blue color is much deeper, as though there's secrets lurking underneath, I sit down for a moment, feeling comfort and security in the solid base of my boat.

As the night rolls in, the overcast sky begins to match the water and I feel completely surrounded by darkness, and completely alone. I head to the other end of the boat to tighten one of the ropes and I completely miss a step. Before I know it, I'm gasping for a breath and trying to tread water. I gulp down several mouthfuls of the sea, panicking as the cold slows my limbs down. I look around me for something to grab onto, now realizing the importance of a security line. As the water sloshes over me, I realize that some of the peaks that just seem to be waves about to break aren't waves at all—they're fins. In every direction I look there seems to be another one, like peaks in a mountain range. I scramble towards the boat, barely able to feel my limbs. My hands slip as I try to find anything substantial to grip onto, avoiding looking at what lurks in the darkness behind me. Although it feels like a long haul, I'm certain I pull myself back onto the boat within a few seconds. I lie there for a few minutes, panting, baffled by my luck.

The next morning, I sail north towards Oman, it takes me a while to digest how close I was to death the night before, I grow concerned for what's in store for me next. I arrive in the city of Salalah and as I approach the port, I can see a few locals beginning to gather. They watch me with intrigue, and I feel

outcasted; I seem to be the only foreigner here. When I arrive,

they begin to talk to me, taking it in turns to take my hand or put

theirs out. They start to claim I need to pay port fees, but there

are inconsistencies in price and I'm almost certain they see me as

a wealthy foreigner. I tell them I need to make some

arrangements first and, eventually, they reluctantly agree.

I find a hostel I can stay in for the night and settle on a top

bunk. Below me there is a young girl, she freely leaves her

backpack, no doubt full of belongings and money, open and in

reach. I think of her ignorance and how she can trust others. She

must have made the assumption that I'm not desperately

interested in her money, let alone a criminal. I wait until the

middle of the night and climb down to use the bathroom. On my

return I notice everyone else in the room is sleeping soundly, so I

take the opportunity to rummage through her bag. Altogether,

she only seems to have 25 dollars, but it's money I'm in

desperate need of, so I take it. I'm about to get back into bed

when I consider the prospect of the girl waking up to find her

money gone. No doubt she'd interrogate everyone in the room. I

make the decision to head back to the port and begin sailing, that way I can avoid negotiating with the locals over port fees as well.

I take very little time gathering together what I'd brought with me to the hostel and hurry back to the port. I feel that I stand out here as the only foreigner, so I rush back to my boat as fast as I can, afraid again that they'll make the assumption that I'm rich. When I eventually reach the boat, I untie it as fast as I can and then begin to set sail. I start heading eastward, with India in my sights.

It takes what feels like a little longer to get there this time; perhaps because the end doesn't seem so far away and my desperation as I reach where I need to be is only increasing.

I am extremely thirsty when I arrive and once I've sourced some water, I begin to take in the scenery. Goa is perhaps the most beautiful of the places I have stopped at so far–that might be because of the relief I feel after finally arriving. The beachfront is coated in lush green palm trees; each one looks like it's been naturally sculpted to perfection. The soft sand is warm and comforts my feet as I wander around with no real plan of where to go. The people flattened out, absorbing the last of the day's sun, are so still that they seem to be like part of the landscape. There's beach huts in every color that line the border where the beach meets the road, almost every single one has been opened up, revealing clutter inside. I notice a pretty looking girl dash out of one hut, almost dancing instead of running, and she throws her head back to let out a laugh of pure delight. Her giggle is completely captivating; it is sweet and silky like honey and I'm drawn to her immediately.

I sit on the beach for a few hours, sifting sand through my fingers until I eventually find the courage to go and speak to the girl–her friends left a few minutes ago.

"Do you speak English?" She looks up at me with wide, bright eyes.

"A little. It's not perfect."

"You're doing well so far. Where are you from? I would guess somewhere in Europe from your accent."

"Russia, although it has been a while since I have been home."

"Me too." I say, and I proceed to tell her the story of my journey so far.

We talked until the sun set and began to rise again. It was only when she asked me where I planned to go from Goa that I remembered the entire purpose of my journey. There were several moments where I felt like an entirely different man: there's so much distance between me right now, feeling euphoric, and the person who lay in bed until he was sobering, reading messages from a former girlfriend. It's been a long time since she ignored my message and as

I sit, taking in the sun and the joy this Russian girl, Aleksandra, is giving me, I can't say I miss her.

After a few days together in Goa, myself and Aleksandra decide to set sail together. She seems to have a lot more money than me but doesn't mind my humble sailing boat. After re-provisioning and topping up the tanks with water and fuel, I set a course for the Andaman Sea.

My last passage from India to Malaysia is extra pleasant, just a light wind closed hauled and a pretty flat sea. We arrive in Penang and by now we're completely besotted by one another.

The evening begins to creep in, and we find Chulia Street in George Town. It's littered with bars, tables and people; all mingled together. Whilst it initially seems crowded, once we start to walk through it seems to widen and welcome us–the crowd engulfing us. We start to hop between bars. Despite them being packed tightly together, each one is distinctive with its own individual smells and sounds. We buy a variety of drinks and a little food and the night turns hazy.

I don't recall losing Aleksandra, or exactly how much alcohol we consumed, but I'm stumbling down the street, perhaps shouting I'm not too sure. There are two ladies lingering outside a massage parlor, both puffing on cigarettes. I make the assumption that they work there and are on their break. One seems familiar, I rub my eyes as if to sober them up but I am unsure of whether it's my imagination. She looks like a girl I was in love with for a very long time. In fact I don't think I ever fell out of love with her, just accepted we couldn't be together. I grow more certain that it's her.

"My love, my darling!"

"Excuse me?" She responds, blankly.

"I have found you, after all this time."

"Are you lost?" I'm not really paying attention to what she's saying anymore.

"Come with me, I'll take care of you now. We are meant to be together."

"What's he on about?" She mutters to her friend.

"I'm telling you I love you and I'm here to save you!"

"What's going on over here?" Two police officers interrupt.

They begin to ask me why I'm talking to the girls; I stumble on my words as I try to explain my situation–they only seem interested when I mention that I'm trying to rescue her. Within a few hours, my ordeal becomes a bit of a sensation. I find myself talking to journalists and reporters who exaggerate every word I say. They tell me that the girls were foreign and forced into working at the massage parlors. They keep telling me I've done an amazing thing and that I'll be remembered as a hero. I thank them, becoming more unsure of what I actually did as I sober up. The girl does not become any less beautiful though and I start to imagine a life with her. However, I can't find her.

My time alone allows me to reflect on the things I have done. I think about my boat; except it's not my boat. I've not really thought about my German neighbor and how he might have reacted. Perhaps I could return to Europe, give him his boat

back and go from there. Money is running low but it seems I'll
always find a way.

I begin untying my boat when the girl returns; everything is
coming together! Then suddenly a man appears from behind her
and takes her hand, she looks at me shamefully and
apologetically. I understand she has her own life to live and we
bid each other goodbye.

I set off again, with no real goal of where to go from here. I don't
feel like I have a proper home anymore, I suppose my boat is my
home now, and if this is where I spend the rest of my life,
however long it may be, then so be it.

CAFÉ LISBON

In September last year, I was in Washington with my friend Fritz. He's the kind of person who's always in a good mood. I have never seen Fritz sad or depressed. He succeeds in everything in life. It's nice that there are such people!

One evening we went out for dinner in a small restaurant next to a Casino mall. What was served was excellent. After dessert, I ordered a coffee and a French cognac, all European. As we sat outside, I was overcome by the desire for a cigar.

"Do you have any?" I asked the restaurant's Chinese manager.

"No, unfortunately, not," was his answer. "We'd be hanged," he said with a sense of humor. "But I know a bar nearby where they have cigars—the Cafe Lisbon. Go out here, then turn left, then right at the next intersection and then left again on the next street. There you'll find Cafe Lisbon. You can't miss it."

I thanked him for the good advice. We paid and left. We found Cafe Lisbon without a problem. The directions given by the restaurant owner had been correct.

At the entrance of the well-kept place, which was open to the outside on this warm September night, we were welcomed by a European-looking patron. He gave us a winning smile as if we were his very best old friends.

"Erminio is my name. And what is yours?"

"I am Paul. My friend's name is Fritz," I told him. "Do you have cigars?"

"Yes, of course! Lots of cigars. Cubans and others. Would you like a Montecristo?"

"Yes, I would. Number four, please."

"You got it, boss," was his answer. "Head to the bar now. You'll find what you're looking for."

The bar was long and crowded. We could hardly find a gap to reach the bar. Soon our two cigars were there waiting for us there. I ordered another coffee and cognac. Fritz took a beer. Soon I was alone at a small bar table, from where I could watch the whole restaurant. Straight ahead of me was the bar, behind me the actual restaurant. Some people were still eating, although it was already half-past ten in the evening.

Where was Fritz? He had gone to the toilet. But where was he now? To my astonishment, I saw him standing at the bar with a blond lady. He toasted with her. Then he kissed her

on the cheeks, and very gently, on the mouth. I couldn't
believe my eyes. Next to him stood a man of about fifty-seven
who seemed to be with the blond woman but hardly took any
notice of what Fritz was doing. *Other countries, other
customs,* I thought to myself.

Opposite me was an Englishman holding court, who must
have been in his forties or fifties. He drank one beer after the
other and saluted me from afar. I left my bar table and walked
towards him. I cheered to him, the big pot-bellied brandy glass
in my hand.

"What are you doing here in Washington?" he asked me.
"Politics?" Washington is full of politicians and lobbyists.

"No. I'm European. I'm here on a visit."

"That's good," nodded the Englishman. "We need
friendship between the Old and New Continents. Do you like
the women here?"
The stranger squeezed a young or young-at-heart woman, pale,
blond and blue-eyed, who looked like a living copy of Marilyn
Monroe. "By the way, this is Jane. And this gentleman is a
European, who hasn't told me his name yet."

"Delighted," I said to Jane and shook her hand. Then I also shook hands with the Englishman. "My name is Paul. What is your name?"

"Well, it's a bit complicated," said the stranger. "I am the son of an English lord. If that's enough for you. Call me Harry that will do. I'm here to build a racetrack for Formula One in Las Vegas. Big thing." He took another sip of beer. "But forget all that. The only thing that matters in this goddamn world is women. Women like Jane." He pressed the beautiful one to himself again, who put up with his strong embrace, not looking as though she liked it, or maybe just didn't care.

Then I returned to my little table. I longed for a sip of coffee. As time passed, the place emptied. Fritz was not quite aware that flirting can be a double-edged sword in America. Anyone who knew him would know that he didn't care anyway. In the meantime, he had already made a pass at a Latino beauty who had round, dark eyes and looked very different. She was also well dressed. Soon he was sitting at a table with her and waved me over. I sat down there as well.

"This is my friend Pablo," he introduced me. "And this is Juanita from Mexico who works here in Washington."

I shook hands with the young woman and exchanged a few words with her. But then quite unexpectedly, Juanita turned back to Fritz.

There was a blond gentleman in his fifties at our table who stood out because of his peach-red jacket. The man looked incredibly sad and tired as if he was about to die. 'Tired of life' crossed my mind. I introduced myself to the man.

"My name is Hans," he answered. "Hans from Sweden." He paused. "I have a house here in Washington. I have several houses in Sweden. I have a house in Gstaad. I have houses everywhere."

"That's wonderful," I answered.

"That's what you think," was his answer. "But houses, like women, only cause problems."

He looked at Jane, who had now come to our table. She had finally broken away from Harry, the English lord's son.

Hans pointed at Jane with an eerily tired gesture. "Do you see this wonderful young woman? I love her. But she wants nothing to do with me. That's a pity."

Jane patted his hand. She looked at him with a perfect Marilyn Monroe smile, coupled with an eerily sharp look.

"Nonsense darling. Of course, I love you too. I love you a lot.
But in a different way. Understand that!"

Hans sighed, took a long sip from his whisky glass and
turned back to me. "You see, this is how a cruel woman
speaks. She wants nothing to do with me but loves me anyway.
Have you ever understood how a woman works?"

Jane had heard all this but kept looking at him with a
sweet smile that was as clear as a still, pure lake.

"Of course women are different from men," I now tried to
comfort Hans, "but there must be some way you can get along
with Jane."

"If only I could find it," sighed Hans and turned back to
his whisky glass.

Jane and Juanita said goodbye. They were going to
another bar. Hans waved goodbye. He was too tired to do
anything more. Jane voiced a tender farewell to Hans and he
received an enchanting smile and a big kiss on the cheek.
That's the way Marilyn must have kissed, I thought. Hans was
now no longer responsive. I said goodbye to him. Together
with Fritz, I went back to the hotel.

THE GIRL FROM THE SALVATION ARMY

Of course, the eighties were the best in old Berlin, as far as I remember. At that time Berlin was still a divided city, flourishing economically and sinking into the mire at the same time. But it was also the time of personal freedom, of openness, perhaps even of free love.

I remember that stupid hat that sat on top of her braided dark blond hair was the first thing I noticed about Iris. And the dark-blue uniform she came up to me in. Of course, I didn't know her name was Iris at the time. She was holding a sheet of paper with the lurid title *War Cry*.

"What *are you* selling?" she wanted to know.

I held up the well-known street magazine that I had been selling around the central station for two years.

She smiled. "Wanna swap?"

I shook my head. "Sorry, I make my living selling this paper. Of the sixty-one people who pay for it, I get 50 pennies, and I need those pennies badly as a welfare recipient."
I held out the cards to her. She nodded and reached into her pocket that contained a whole stack of her newspaper. She

pulled out a wallet and gave me a two-coin. "Keep the change."

Then she handed me her paper. "But don't throw it away. Read it. Bye."

I watched her as she walked on.

Suddenly she turned around again and smiled. "Jesus loves you!"

Jesus loves you. Sure, I thought, of course. That's why I've been doing so well for the last five years. First my divorce, then the work-accident with the complicated fracture and eight weeks later my expulsion from Meyers Construction, the company for which I was employed for almost five years with the most dangerous renovation work in the still very much in-need-of-renovation West Berlin.

"We are sorry, but with a serious injury like yours, which will never really heal properly, even if you only work for the company as a driver, you will no doubt be required to help with the loading." That was it.

I no longer had an apartment of my own either, instead, I shared a flat with three other men. I had fifteen square meters to myself. We shared the kitchen and a bathroom. *But Jesus loves you, of course.* Nice, but that girl was a bit unworldly

When in the evening, I had counted the takings and made myself comfortable on my old but cozy couch with a bottle of beer, I grabbed the *War Cry* and leafed through it. At that moment the scales fell from my eyes, as they say. That girl was in the Salvation Army! I had only moved to Berlin three months earlier, so I had not yet come into contact with these people.

I couldn't help smiling. If I happened to meet the young woman again, I would ask her some really good questions. I was good at that. In Berlin, I had made a preacher sweat once.

The opportunity presented itself a week later when I saw the little "Soldier of Christ' — one of three million worldwide according to the *War Cry* — again on the cow dam in front of the department store. This time, however, she was not alone. She was singing a pious song together with some other uniformed men who accompanied her with a guitar. After the last verse, Iris broke away from the small troop and came towards me. She handed me a flyer.

"If you feel like it, come by our place sometime. We have a service at a quarter past eight and after that our coffee bar opens. My name is Iris, by the way."

Iris, a powerful Greek name, flashed through my mind. I couldn't help smiling.

She raised an eyebrow. "What's so funny?"

"Oh, nothing," I replied and introduced myself as well.

"Peter Schmidt. Where can I find your club?"

"Jesus lives in the Bahnhof Zoo', was written on the large sign above the entrance of the old station vaults, where the Salvation Army had its headquarters. This is how I had read it in the W*ar Cry.* I had missed the service — Iris, seemed a little disappointed about it — but I never say no to a cup of coffee. And the coffee bar, which quickly filled with men and women, was a really cozy place.

"Say, Max..." Iris poured herself a cup of coffee.

Ah, and now the first attempt of conversion was probably coming. Nothing. Instead, that night we talked about everything but God. Strange. Wasn't that the point of the invitation? Okay, at one point Iris briefly touched on the subject when she talked about her work and about what the Salvation Army did — from caring for the elderly in need of care and giving out food and clothing to advising debtors to helping addicts. I must admit I was impressed.

"And why are you doing all this?" was what I wanted to know from Iris. That was my first mistake.

"Because I have seen that God loves me." She smiled. "And now I just want to pass on some of that love. Very practical. There are enough people out there who just talk about it. What I like about the Salvation Army is that they do something about the need. That's why I'm here."

Well, I had no objection to that. Instead, that night I felt something I hadn't felt in ten years. I was in love.

When we said goodbye, I asked Iris if we could see each other again soon.

"You mean here?"

I shook my head. "I was actually thinking about taking a walk after work. Maybe one of these parks around here."

She hesitated.

"Or do you have a boyfriend?"

"No, that's not it. But I don't actually do this sort of thing."

I wasn't ready to give up that easily. "You invited me for coffee, now I'd like to return the favor with a bratwurst or a chicken sandwich!"

She smiled. "Chicken sandwich sounds good."

"Saturday afternoon?"

She nodded. "But only until seven. Then I've got to be back at the station entrance with another Salvation Army man, to hand out papers."

Iris works in Berlin's most wicked train station, behind every corner, there were johns, prostitutes and sex shops, and there were drunks in every corner. A strange place to work. If someone had told me that...

On Saturday, we met at Bahnhof Zoo, and from there we took a two-hour walk towards the Zoo. We enjoyed the wonderful summer weather and talked about everything. Time flew by and when we said goodbye to each other, we each knew each other's life story, favorite music and favorite food! By the way, today was the first time Iris had given up her uniform, and I liked her even more.

When we shook hands — I would have much rather kissed her — she suddenly said,

"You could actually accompany me this evening. Or do you have other plans?"

I shook my head. "Not really, but is that even possible? I don't belong to your club, after all."

"Oh, that's all right." She smiled. "I'll be right there with you."

So that Saturday night, I went up and down the cow's perineum with Iris, and Herbert, an older man. I had definitely fallen in love with this young woman, who had only entered my life a few days earlier. My admiration for Iris grew from hour to hour.

Even though not everyone to whom she offered her newspaper was happy to accept it or engage in conversation, Iris remained friendly. There had to be something to her faith, after all.

Just before midnight, all the newspapers were distributed, and I was dog-tired.

"Will you join me for a glass of juice or something?" I asked and was quite surprised when Iris nodded. So we continued our intense conversation in my room.

No, we didn't end up in bed. We waited until our wedding night, six months later. After all, my wife is a person of principles.

By the way, we still distribute the *War Cry* together. And not only in the run-down station district, but everywhere. We have no borders now.

THE LONDON MARATHON

It was by chance that I was in London last April. It was the last Sunday of the month when the marathon is traditionally held, attracting tens of thousands of participants and spectators. I was in the second category. Together with my Swiss friend, I went to the end of the small park in Blackheath in the morning around eleven o'clock, where the numerous Swiss runners had set up their so-called Swiss Curve.

The charming lady at the Swiss Consulate General in London immediately gave me a red and white T-shirt with a large Swiss cross in the middle. Unfortunately, I was too late for the distribution of the racy caps with the Swiss colors, which was not tragic, as the day was mild and beautiful, and the sun was not burning down on us.

The over thirty thousand runners had already started at ten o'clock to cover the distance of over 42 kilometers.

Our Swiss place on the marathon course was at kilometer 33. Not very far from the finish line, which would finally bring salvation to the runners, after crossing the Embankment to Parliament Square. This meant that we could only expect to see the runners by the beginning of the afternoon. On a small table, we offered glasses with coke and fruit. We wanted to offer the runners, especially the Swiss contingent, some refreshments when they arrived at some point.

I passed the time talking to Swiss people who lived in London. I soon realized that I was dealing with a large number of very successful businessmen who loved London and Switzerland equally, and who had one thing above all else, success in life. That's what life is all about in the end. Next to the Swiss stand, a big band from Barbados and Tobago had settled down, chasing hot rhythms into the deep blue late autumn day, which was still part of the Indian Summer. The boys and girls created terrific sounds from the oil barrels. Eventually, they danced to the music, giving rise to a small carnival.

Finally, there was movement on the previously empty street. Police cars and publicity trucks drove by. A camera team filmed the spectators. The Mayor of London drove by in a classic open vehicle. People cheered.

At last, the first runner came into view, then others, first only a handful, then suddenly a large mass. The Swiss Embassy ran past, accompanied by a small bodyguard proudly carrying a Swiss flag.

We were suddenly very busy at the stand. I was cutting bananas, and another Swiss guy kept on refilling coke while his colleague put new cups on the table. Our customers were by no means all Swiss. But that didn't matter at all.

The main thing was that we were of service to these hungry and thirsty runners, which was gratefully acknowledged. There was already some publicity for Switzerland, as some colleagues from the Consulate General busily waved Swiss flags and rang cowbells. Those who kept their eyes closed could truly imagine themselves in the Swiss Alps. We were in Harlem, where it was teeming with black children who enthusiastically wore Swiss T-shirts and red and white caps.

Sometime between three and four o'clock in the afternoon, the race came to an end. There were now only a few isolated runners who were simply walking as they would on a Sunday walk. But many looked terrible, sweaty and exhausted. Pity was stirring in me. The things that man does to himself! I spotted an old, thin woman who really looked like a mummy — only skin and bones, but I quickly realized she was a marathon runner because of her sports shoes and T-shirt. She was totally exhausted. Suddenly she came right up and looked at me with a strange but gentle expression. Wordlessly I gave her coke and banana chips. I swallowed at the sight of her and cleared my throat.

"I admire you."

Her old eyes flashed, suddenly she seemed to awaken.

"Are you sure about that?" she asked.

"Well, let me ask you, why are you doing this Marathon?"

"To show and prove faith."

I shook my head slightly. "At your age, you don't need to prove anything."

She took one step closer, then pointed her finger at the sky.

"No for me, for Him." She nodded at me again, then slowly walked down the empty street.

Later, I returned with my friend to the house where he lived, where I had rented a room next door. We said goodbye.

"Will we see you again next year at Swiss Curve at the London Marathon? I'd be delighted."

"I'll let you know later," I answered somewhat sheepishly.

A few months later, my friend called again. "So, I'll see you next April in London at the marathon?"

"Yes, and I'm going to compete," I replied proudly.

"You want to run. Are you sure?"

"Absolutely."

He paused on the phone for several seconds. "May I ask you why you're doing this?"

"I'm doing it for HIM, because of my faith, my friend."

I don't know any more than you do David. Livia was pounding at her laptop keyboard, the words tripping over themselves in her mind faster than she could type the email. *I'm pretty sure I only got the email by mistake. It was meant for Miranda. Have you heard of this man, "Julian'? What does he want with my sixteen-year-old daughter anyway, can't he get enough chicks being a millionaire?*

Livia slammed the send button and leaned back. She ran her fingers through her brown hair a few times. What a way to wake up, opening an email from a millionaire she never met who was—apparently—dating Miranda.

And the mention of Devil's Island? An eerie enough name to send her back to David. They hadn't spoken for years since the divorce, and Livia would have preferred it that way. But while Livia had kept custody of Miranda, David got the *Chaste*, and Livia had a feeling the sailboat would be very useful very shortly.

The laptop rang and Livia lunged forward. Was the email sent from the island? Could she get Anthony to trace its source. "How are you holding up?" it asked.

Of course, Anthony, David' sailing friend. He was a satellite technician for the Department of Defense. Livia railed off a response—*Yes, get Anthony on the case right away*—and leaped up off the couch to begin packing a rucksack. She already had a plan in her head.

An hour later found Livia back at the computer, compulsively refreshing her email as her leg bounced up and down. Next to her sat an overstuffed bag. Her searches for "Devil's Island" had come up with nothing but cheap pirate stories, not even a rumour about a real island with that name.

She thought back to when she had dressed for this expedition. A middle-aged woman in snug jeans and a pale blue windbreaker. Livia, not exactly action hero material, could feel something was off. If she couldn't get to Miranda, who would?

Livia read through David's email. "Anthony says that Devil's Island is just off Honduras, near the island of Roatan. No flights are available." She also searched the dark web and found some crazy shit; a history of cults, shipwrecks; not at all good.

"Do you want to stay here tonight and talk it over?

Livia was already snapping the computer shut as she read the last line. Honduras, that was a short trip from the Caymans, and she was going there anyways for their sailboat the *Chaste*. Snatching up the bag, she stalked off toward the door, fully prepared to burst out into the night and head straight for the airport. Miranda was her daughter, dammit, not even a creep with an island could change that. With her hand on the knob, something stopped her. A little tickle in her heart, maybe. Livia turned slowly back to the laptop.

Miranda was David' daughter too.

With a breathy sigh, Livia let the bag drop and moved back to the computer.

Livia marched down the dock with her bag over her shoulder, fully aware that David was keeping a few paces behind her. The weather in the Caymans was usually sunnier, but today the sky was a soft grey. Overhead seagulls screamed, threatening all the pleasure craft below with a fecal divebombing. "Take a right," David called out.

With mechanical coldness, Livia rotated. As she turned, she got a glimpse of David. He had squeezed himself into a nicer shirt and pants than Livia had ever seen him wear during their marriage. Even his mop of hair had been brushed back, though insistently untrimmed. Definitely trying to make a good impression. Livia was privately seething at David. They were here together for one thing: Miranda. In her mind, Livia was planning a dozen scenarios and rescue attempts, bracing herself for what a punch to the gut might feel like, taking inventory of what keys on her chain she could have ready to hold in her fist. Meanwhile her oaf of an ex-husband was trying to woo her with khakis.

Ahead, at the end of the dock, the *Chaste* was waiting. Livia slowed down to take a good look at the 26-footer bobbing in the water. It was about a decade old by now, though there were hardly any marks of wear and tear. This rather small boat was graceful, elegant, with a cropped stern and a narrow clipper bow.

It all didn't matter to her. "I never liked sailing," she said as David caught up.

"I know, that's why I made friends with Anthony. Look how that worked out." He smiled at her and extended a hand toward the boat. "Shall we? I've paid to keep her in good condition. Just as soon as this poor weather passes, we can push off."

"What?" Livia rounded on David. "No, we're going now."

David' face blanched. "Liv, there's going to be a storm. Just look!"

"First, my name is not Liv. Second, we don't know if Miranda's safe! I've got a bad feeling that…" Livia's voice faded as she glanced around for eavesdroppers, "that she's ended up in sex slavery. This Julian asshole sends a chill down my spine. You should have read his email. It sounded pleasant, but there was this sharpness under the surface. An authority."

"Jesus Christ," was all David could get out.

Livia wordlessly led them onto the *Chaste*, where she settled behind the wheel as David began unmooring them. Under Livia's control, the engine rumbled to life, and with an easterly blowing at their backs they coasted into the sea.

"Are we going to spend this whole trip in passive-aggressive silence?" David asked as Livia turned them windward.

"Main sail," she replied.

As he pulled the rope, David said, "Fine, but we need to talk about what we're doing on this Devil's Island."

Livia began to bring them around, the wind catching her clothes. Now they were pointed into the sun. "Unfurl the spinnaker." David complied. The sails billowed out and the *Chaste* began cutting through the water at good speed. "We're going in there and demanding Miranda back. If anything is suspicious, we'll threaten to call the cops."

"And you think Julian will listen?"

A cloud passed over the sun and cast them into shade.

"Maybe you were right about the storm," Livia said.

"Nah, I'm sure it'll be fine." David was smiling placidly at Livia from the bow.

"You're such a doormat," she said.

"Put your safety harness on", but she ignored him. She didn't want to listen to that kind of crap anymore.

The rain came before sunset. The *Chaste* was not built for the high seas, but that was where Livia was steering her. All around them raindrops pelted into ever growing waves with a sound like gunfire. David was sheltering near Livia's ankles, ducked out of the way. The skies were ash grey now.

"Still on course!" David hollered over the roaring wind.

Livia was about to respond when she noticed something out of the corner of her eye. A massive wave was cresting, blocking the horizon entirely from view. "Hold on!" she screamed.

The wave slammed into them like a tanker truck. Livia went crashing into the wheel and felt the wind get knocked out of her. Below, David did a half-somersault backwards as the water lifted him off his feet.

"The spinnaker!" Livia desperately pointed ahead, where a line had snapped, leaving the spinnaker to snap around in the wind.

David choked out a lungful of seawater. "Leave it, let the waves carry us!" he managed.

The bow of the ship was yanked up by another wave, the wind speed again increased dramatically to over thirty-five knots off the port bow. David shortened the mainsail and hung on for another wild ride.

Livia caught a shadow on the horizon. "There! That looks like land." Planting her feet to keep from slipping again, she strained against the wheel until she felt the *Chaste* begin to turn. "David, take the sail down!" She whipped her head around. "David?" she shouted. He was nowhere to be seen. Just as she turned back to the horizon, a crack of lightning split the sky and Livia's ears were blasted by thunder. Suddenly she heard something like a snapping sound and then she felt a sharp pain. It felt like a whip had struck her entire face and pulled the skin off. She screamed in pain, but still could hear him yelling. "Livia! Oh my god! The bowsprit has been ripped out!"

She grabbed a piece of metal, she had to get up, but she could not see as the blood was running down her forehead into her eyes. Suddenly a wall of water crashed onto the deck like a force from hell. Her feet lifted off the deck and she saw the sailboat fall away as she was lifted into the air. The boat was leaning and there was no floor below her feet. So, this is what it feels like when a boat capsizes.

David had his safety harness on, but the wave smashed him against the bow mast with such a force that he thought he had broken his spine.

Livia felt the water and realized she was surrounded by water and halfway under it. The cold water was sinking in. Her clothes were clinging to her body and her throat was burning. Her hands were flailing, and her eyes were closing.

Livia woke up with a dry throat. Sunlight was fighting its way through her eyelids. Painfully, she opened her eyes and looked around. A foot-long spike of the *Chaste*'s mast was sticking out of the sand next to her head. She was laying on a beach, sun overhead. And a few yards away…

"David!" Livia gasped. She tried to run but her legs were wobbly and she dropped into the sand. Instead she crawled over. David was immobile, face down in the sand. "You need to get up, David. Move! Come on!" Livia dug her hands under him and with great effort flipped him onto his back.

David let out a gravelly wheeze and jack-knifed up. Livia knelt over panting as David coughed water up, out onto the beach. "Where are we?" Livia asked, squinting around at the beach. It didn't look large at all, only a mile before the beach curved away inland where a bright green jungle was visible.

"Welcome to Devil's Island," said a strange voice. Livia spun around on her knees. A man with lanky blonde hair was standing over them, dressed in a toga laid over grey army fatigues. "Your presence is requested."

Two similarly dressed men emerged from the jungle. As they approached, the first man kept a knife-sharp smile on his face. Livia and David were both pulled roughly to their feet by the two men, and the group began to march into the jungle.

Livia's legs ached, but the men in uniform urged her on. Soon, a white shape peeked through the jungle ahead. Livia could hear music, and voices. They rounded a corner, and she could see it was a mansion tucked away in the heart of the island.

It was very modern, made of bleached white concrete with a blocky, geometric design.

"In you go," said the first man in uniform.

With a shove from behind, Livia and David were released. With a quick look to confirm David wasn't seriously injured, Livia took the lead and moved into the mansion's entry hall. It was a long corridor lit with flickering light. In the shadows against the wall, Livia could see more men in uniforms, these ones armed with AR15s. David moved up next to her and leaned into her ear. "Stick close to me," he whispered.

"Only if you're going to wherever Miranda is," Livia hissed back, and began strutting forward.

None of the men in uniform showed any emotion. Ahead Livia could hear the music and chatter getting louder. Finally, a wide set of doors came into view. As she approached—David on her heels—a man stepped forward and opened one door.

Through it strolled a very tall, muscular man. Livia could see his muscles because he wore only a toga, and loosely wrapped at that. He had a hard jaw, and a beautiful mane of gold hair on which a silver olive laurel sat. Livia was struck with the image of a Roman emperor, although one of the insane ones. The man's eyes rolled back and forth wildly as he looked her up and down. "Yes, yes. Good of you to join us. I hope your shipwreck was not so bad, as shipwrecks go, of course." The man's head shot back in a cruel laugh that sounded like breaking ice.

"Are you Julian?" Livia snapped. "Where's my daughter?"

"Who the hell are you? You know me by name?" Julian seemed not to hear Livia.

"That is interesting. Come," he gestured to the doors, "join my feast. Eat of my bread and enjoy the comforts of my home. Goodness knows I've sampled some of your comforts."

"You bastard! Where's Miranda?"

But Julian only laughed again and slipped behind the massive door. Livia leapt forward after him, but the view behind the door stopped her dead.

It was a massive dining hall, with a vaulted ceiling supported by a hundred marble pillars. It could have been a Roman palace. All around were guests, plucking grapes off serving platters and dancing in place. Julian had disappeared into the crowd.

Livia began to wander into the room. "Wait, stop!" David said, grabbing Livia's arm. She shot him a dark look and he immediately let her go. "I just mean, shouldn't we be careful?"

"You be cautious, I'll find Miranda. Deal?" Livia began to weave between guests.

The guests were dressed in spotless tuxedos and shimmering evening gowns, all of them in bright colors so that it was as if Livia was shouldering her way between birds of paradise. She saw guests gently placing fingers in each others' mouths. Some laughed hard enough their champagne glasses dropped from their hands, smashing on the ground. On accident, she knocked into one woman who simply spun in place like she was weightless. "What is this…" Livia said to herself. She went up to a lucid looking gentleman in a scarlet waistcoat. "Hello, what is this feast for?"

The man chuckled and waved her away. "No, answer me!" Only more laughing. Livia realized the man's eyes were almost as red as his waistcoat, and his pupils were pinpricks. "You're no use," Livia informed the man with a shove.

For what felt like an hour she dodged through the guests. Miranda was nowhere to be seen. Worse yet, the feast hall didn't seem to have exits. Livia pushed through a pair of vapid women and banged a fist against a smooth marble wall. There was no echo. She was definitely trapped. Livia leaned her head against the wall, and suddenly noticed how tight her head felt. In shock, she looked down at her hands. They were wavering in front of her, fading in and out of focus. Livia spun, but her knees buckled and she crashed onto the floor facedown. Guests around her began laughing. "Help me," she said weakly. Her eyes were closing on their own. She thought she could taste blood in her mouth. "Please, find Miranda…"

When she woke up, Livia felt bars pressing onto her back. It took her a moment to realize her eyes had in fact opened, but that she was just in a pitch-black room. Slowly, she got to her feet.

She was inside a large cage, the steel bars almost as thick around as her arm. It was positioned against a dark wall—Livia reached an arm out of the cage and felt the wall was rough stone. She must be inside a cave of some sort. To either side, more cages stretched out in a semicircle. A few were occupied, other frightened people coming to their senses, but most were empty. The cages faced an open area in the cave's centre, beyond which stretched a hallway cut into the rock. Livia shivered, half from the chill of the cave and half from a growing dread.

While looking, Livia's eyes suddenly latched onto a figure slumped a little way down the hallway. She slammed forward into the cage bars, pounding them with her palm. "David! Are you alright? David, wake up!"

David didn't stir. Livia couldn't see any blood on him, but the cave was so dim it was hard to see.

Behind David burst a line of light, another set of double doors opening. Leading a group of people came Julian, this man was dressed like a Roman emperor in a golden breastplate and with a deep red tunic. He had added a golden crown onto his head to complement his laurel, completing the look of a crazed king. Following him came a dozen men dressed the same, though not so luxuriously. Among them Livia recognized the sharp face of the uniformed man who had grabbed her and David on the beach.

The soldiers spread out into a line in the cave's centre. There were more footsteps from the door, but Livia's view was now cut off as Julian paced around the chamber, pausing at each cage. He passed by Livia and stopped. "Keep your head about you now," he murmured through a smirk, "I will not tolerate interruptions."

He stalked off. Livia bit her lip and dug her nails into the metal of the cage. The other people now came into view: a dozen young girls, dressed in stained linen tunics with hoods over their faces. Livia could see their chests heaving as a few sobbed quietly. Their hands were bound with hemp rope. One by one, they were led to kneel next to a soldier and drop onto their hands and knees.

"Countrymen!" Julian's voice boomed out, echoing around the cave. Livia flinched slightly; the voice seemed louder than life. "Today we inaugurate the new era of our glorious empire! I, the lost God, have to come to you so that we may march hand-in-hand into a new golden era. These cattle," and as he spoke, he waved to the girls, "are my tribute. Slaves captured from my vanquished enemies. Their sacrifice will restore my divinity." Julian reached a hand between the folds of his tunic. "They shall receive my sacred semen and be beheaded!"

"No!" Livia screamed. Her throat felt like it was tearing as she shrieked. "Stop! Kill me instead, not them! Get away from them!"

"Gag that cunt!" Julian commanded.
A pair of soldiers came over to Livia's cage, where she was thrashing against the bars. One roughly grabbed her hair and pulled, slamming her head into the hard metal, one, twice. Livia saw flashes of white and her breath caught. The soldiers wrapped a piece of linen around her mouth, gagging her. One gripped her wrists and bound them with coarse rope, cutting into her skin.

They threw Livia away, and she fell onto her back, panting for breath.

"Begin," she heard Julian say.

Livia's body was a mix of fire and ice. She was sure now she could feel blood from some wound trickling over her face, and the icy iron of the cage was numbing her body as she laid on it. With effort, Livia rolled into a fetal position and looked at the girls.

Julian was shifting the linen tunic up the back of the first girl in the line, kneeling behind her. Livia saw the curve of the girl's buttocks, and Julian began thrusting. The soldier standing nearby ripped the hood off the girl's head, and Livia saw tears streaming down the face of the teenager. The soldier drew a long sword from a scabbard, the razor-sharp metal glinting in the dark of the cave. As Livia watched, breath now coming only in gasps, Julian let out a roar of pleasure, and the soldier's sword swung down. The girl let out a brief scream before it was cut short, and the body collapsed like a ragdoll, blood pouring from the jagged stump of a neck.

"Next," Julian said.

Livia struggled to her feet as the next girl was raped. Julian's face was stony, some unhuman fire burning inside him. The next soldier removed the hood and drew his sword. Livia only got a brief look at the sobbing girl before she made herself look away. She felt, rather than heard, the sword sing through the air and the body drop to the floor.

As she looked back up, Julian's eyes connected with hers. Livia felt a weight drop in her gut. "Take the hood off," Julian ordered.

When the soldier removed the hood, a nest of brunette hair fell out. The girl shakily raised her head, and with horror Livia saw a familiar face. "Miranda! I'm here, mom's here! Stop this you sick maniac! Leave her, not her, just let Miranda go!" The words were coming out garbled through the gag. "Please, please, take me, please," Livia sobbed. She could see Miranda's eyes darting around, looking for an exit. Her daughter, only sixteen. "Please, I'm here, please..."

All of a sudden thunder filled the room. Julian and his soldiers staggered back in shock. Livia dropped to her belly as screams began ringing out, Julian shouting commands, but Livia realized there were other voices, some speaking Spanish. Another boom rang out and it clicked in Livia's head that it wasn't thunder but explosives. At the end of the cave's hallway, the doors opened again, spilling bright light into the cave. Flashlight beams began dancing over the walls. The soldiers began to draw their swords and rush toward the light. And over everything, Julian kept screaming, his arrogant face now broken into a howl of anger. Livia's last image of that cave was Julian's red face almost unhinging at the jaw as he shrieked that his soldiers would die for him, his voice echoing over all the chaos and noise like a desperate dictator in his last breath.

Livia came to consciousness all at once, sitting up in bed so quickly she nearly threw herself forward. A soft voice nearby said, "Whoa, whoa! Hey, it's good, you're safe."

A gentle-looking man in a knit sweater was laying a hand on Livia's shoulder. He looked familiar from somewhere, even as Livia's head spun. Her body hadn't hurt this badly since childbirth… "Miranda!" she cried out.

"Fine. She's fine," the man said.

Suddenly his soft brown eyes connected to a name in Livia's mind. "Anthony?" She leaned back, letting out a breath, and found the bed was raised up. Looking around, they were in a cramped hospital ward, sectioned off by a curtain. Behind the curtain Livia could hear someone speaking Spanish. Anthony was sitting with her.

"Why are you here?"

"After chatting with David, I kept looking up that island. Found some more details, like that a certain millionaire just bought it. I was up all night, digging and digging. There was horrible stuff, black magic, cult ties, human sacrifices. That island is nothing but bad news. Finally, I knew I had to call someone. So, I called everyone. Coast guard, Honduras police, American embassies up and down the Mosquito Coast."

"And Miranda?" Livia realized her voice was hoarse.

"She's shaken, but alive."

"I want to see her."

"You will, but the doctors said you have a concussion and can't walk yet."

But Livia was already climbing out of bed. Her head felt like it would crack open, but the thought of Miranda being nearby got her moving. At the first step, her ankle rolled and she collapsed onto the linoleum floor.

"Hey, hey, please. You need to heal up."

"Miranda…" Livia began crawling towards the gap in the curtains. "Please…"

Anthony was following her, awkwardly trying to lift Livia by the armpits. As she passed into the hallway, she could hear footsteps pounding behind her. Someone was talking quickly in Spanish, and more arms now were lifting her up, dragging her back.

"No, please, Miranda… I need to see her… tell her I'm sorry I wasn't quicker… please…" Livia was gasping and sobbing as Anthony and the nurses dropped her back into her bed. "Tell her… please… Miranda…"

THE BREACH

I had never felt such peace. The gentle sway of the cruise ship upon the Norwegian channels created a mesmerizing effect; with my eyes closed, I could imagine myself in a realm of clouds, or else floating, without body, in the dark, star-ridden void. My earbuds encapsulated me in the sounds of sitar and soft Indian chanting. I began to lose myself. The void, the music, the beautiful Nordic scenery that I unconsciously knew was floating by - all this helped to provide the most relaxing setting for meditation.

It was early March and my vacation along the Norwegian fjords had only just begun. A few nights spent in the mildly bustling heart of Oslo and then I was off, off on the tranquil journey I had so long saved for. Now there was nothing to do but enjoy the peace and quiet.

The jangling sitar in the earbuds gradually faded to the sounds of water softly splashing. The water sound gained momentum and began to roar. My meditation became so deep that I began to drift towards sleep. I sunk deeper and deeper, eventually into a dream. My dreams took me to unimagined places. I saw an island in the distance, surrounded by pirate ships en masse, flying flags of an unknown, confederate nation. In my mind's eye I saw sandcastles of unimaginable height crumble, become tortoise shells, and return to the sea, where a mermaid scooped them to her ample bosom. I dreamt strangely, deep and long, of the old gods and their cohorts who ruled the sea long before maps had charted them.

Suddenly, I was jarred rudely awake. I woke with a gasp and clutched the side of my head, which smarted sharply. My hand came away covered in blood. I was disoriented; I couldn't fathom what had happened. Here I was, meditating and dreaming, when suddenly I was woken, bleeding as if I had been assaulted by one of the weird creatures of my dream-reverie. I was laying on the floor and my clothes were soaking wet. I pulled myself up by hugging the side of the bed, still unbalanced from the wound I had received to the head, and tried desperately to get my bearings. Water seeped steadily in from the cracks between door and hallway. I made my way to the door and jerkily threw it wide, alarm now starting to inhibit basic motor skills.

Water gushed down the hallway in a way I can only describe as wild. It was like the scene from a disaster film; the overhead alarms sounded and cast everything red. The overhead lights flickered, some blown out completely. The sound of the water rushing through the ship was immense; it flooded my senses, its thunderous roar recalling the same sound that I had just a short time ago meditating upon – that had swept me away to the land of dreams.

Slowly I began to make my way down the hall and towards the nearest emergency exit that I knew of. Struggling against the current, I began to become faint, the strength leaving my body the longer I prodded along. I was almost given out when I finally came upon the steep stairs that led up to the exit. But I was not the only one who had made their way to this spot, as a long line of passengers were halted on and around the steps, nobody moving, only grumbling and cursing their luck. Many wore life-vests already, which reassured me, and I began to look around for some crew member in order to secure my own life-vest. There were none to be found. This vast throng of people were all fellow passengers, ranging from small children to the advanced elderly who had wished to look upon the beautiful fjords before they died. The ship began to vibrate in a violent manner, causing a wave of hysteria to work its way through us, as some fell into the churning water and others braced themselves as best they could. I took a young girl by the hand so that she would not slip and tried to give her a reassuring look, though whatever she saw in my eyes only made her begin to cry and beg for her mother.

Ever so slightly, I began to feel the ship roll to its side. It was tipping; this was it. I was experiencing the kind of capsize that one only reads about. My heart began to pound and I was afraid I squeezed the little girl's hand so hard that her cry became a pitched, anxious scream. Just when I thought all was lost, I saw the crew approaching us from the opposite direction wearing red vests, making their way against the frothing current. The lurid red light of the overheard alarms washed over them in rounds and they seemed to come towards us at a snail's pace. When they were within shouting distance, I heard one of the leading crewmen scream,

"There are no more lifeboats. They are all gone! You must jump! Into the ocean with you all! It is your only chance!"

What followed his announcement was utter pandemonium. Parents and children alike began to wail. Even the elderly, who were previously stoic and composed, started to cry, to curse Jesus and Poseidon alike. At some point I lost the girl. I began to push others aside and struggle towards the steps, which was no easy feat given that most were frozen and weighted down by fright, unable to muster the awareness to make way. It was like wading through a crowd of sleeping buffalo. When I eventually reached the top of the stairs I looked out upon dark waters, the near frozen straights of the Norwegian fjords. Let me tell you: I could *see* the cold. I gazed into those steel grey depths and doubted my courage to do it - to take the final plunge.

"Jump, damn you!", I heard someone shout from behind me. Without turning, I began to make my way closer to the edge.

"Jump you damn fool, or I will throw you overboard myself!"

Still I could not. Hesitantly, I began to retrace my steps. Suddenly I felt someone's hand press against the small of my back and I was pushed violently off and into the water.

The last thing I remember was striking the water. It was blinding cold. I gasped in spite of myself and my lungs filled with ice. And then, complete darkness.

All was dark. I drifted in a sea of black, in a place seemingly without current. I did not know if I was up or down, which way was which. Nothing seemed to matter at that point. I rolled in the afterlife, the nothing that is nonexistence. But to my surprise I soon spied distant lights, like strange willow-the-wisps which flitted about in these blank depths. What could it possibly be? I began to feel the bubbling of consciousness and I willed myself towards them, not swimming, but harnessing a kind of locomotion which simply carried me along.

These luminous spots were not willow-the-wisps at all, nor any other strange creature out of a fairy tale. They were lamps, and they illuminated an underground city of shell and coral. Stalagmites soared upwards from the ocean floor in myriad colors, and around them twisted vague spirits – bearded men, nymphs, ghostly sea-sprites. They beckoned me…forever onward…

I was drawing closer. They were the sea god's couriers, guards, and statesmen. And I belonged to their kingdom.

"She is waking up. Oh god, she made it."

I heard the voice as if from a great distance. I opened my eyes and looked about wildly, expecting to be surrounded by those strange denizens of the fjord's bottom. Only they were ordinary people. They were my fellow passengers, gathered and looking down at me. I recognized the interior of my cabin. There was the Degas, the one of the Parisian milliners;

The fire extinguisher attached to the wall.

"Wow, she was really out cold. Are you ok, miss? You must have bumped your head," said an elderly woman as she reached to feel my forehead. "You are bleeding."

A miracle had occurred. I gingerly peeked under my shirt and saw that my bra now consisted of two small tortoise shells, held together by rough twine. I noticed that my hands were somewhat webbed. I wiggled my toes. I had been chosen, had I not?

I'm coming Father.

I shouldered my way through the concerned crowd and made for the emergency exit.

THE DISFIGURED PAINTING

Chapter One

Steven Schmidt blew into his hands and rubbed them

furiously. It was not winter, but the crisp Portland air

was a reminder it was not too far away. Soon he would

head off back to Houlton, Penabscot County after a

long, tedious week attending a Medical conference.

While there was still time to kill, he decided to

investigate Portland's well-known flea markets. He

found himself walking around Flea-For-All. The place

filled with people, chattering and observing a vast

range of items displayed. Steven 's parents filled their

house with all sorts of antiques and passed that love

for antiques to him. His eyes roamed from chairs to

carpets, tables and finally, a group of paintings

casually displayed on the floor that rested against a

bedside table. He frowned at one in particular. He

pried it gently from the rest of paintings. Finding it

lighter than its appearance, he lifted it gently from the

floor with ease. The dark wooden frame housed one of
the ugliest paintings he had ever seen in his life. It was
a portrait of a grotesque looking old woman. Her
sharp eyes blue as the ocean, stared at him, and her
hair gold like leaves in the fall, swirled and danced
with the wind. Her disfigured face was swollen,
covered with infected lesions of yellows and browns.
Her pale skin had red patches, with silvery flaky
scales. Behind her, a bright lake and a gloomy cabin
strangely accentuated her form, fully dressed in black.
At the bottom left corner were the initials *E.L.*

Steven was intrigued. He felt something. He
wanted to know more about this painting, this person.
Who was she? Who was the painter? Who was *E.L*?
There was no date. It looked like something from the
early 1900's. Could it be a kind of plague? Leprosy?
Psoriasis?

"An interesting choice," A gruff voice said
behind him.

Swiftly looking behind, Steven replied. "Uh, yes.
It is. I have never seen a painting like this before."

An elderly man stood tall, hands in his pockets. The buttons of his green and blue-checkered shirt stretched tight across his belly.

"You can take it, if you want." He said.

"Yes, I think I will. But, I don't see a price tag anywhere." Steven turned the painting over a few times searching for it.

"Don't bother. You can just take it." The man's brows furrowed. "I've been trying to get rid of it for almost a year now."

"Are you the owner?"

"I am, name's Bill Mugger. No surprise that nobody wants it."

"Steven ." The men gripped hands in a quick firm handshake. "Do you know anything about this painting?"

Bill shook his head slightly. "I came to open up sometime last year and somebody left it at the door." He sighed. "There was a note. It said to give this to a decent person that comes along. Something to that affect, anyway."

"And, so you hid it?"

"Not at first. When I started losing customers, I hid it away. I guess its bad luck."

"Thank you, Bill . Are you sure I can't pay you for it?"

"Please, just take it. That is payment enough. If you want, why don't you try Antique Arts Gallery? They not far away," He shrugged. "Maybe someone there can help you out."

After a quick glance at the painting carefully wrapped, thanks to Antique Arts Gallery, Steven closed the trunk of his car. His mind filled with unanswered questions, as he thought more about the painting, and what the curator had told him. His desire to find out more about the painting grew stronger. This was going to be a very long drive back to Houlton.

****

Steven rubbed his hair with a towel as he left the steaming, hot bathroom behind him. There was

nothing more refreshing than a hot shower after a
four-hour drive, and a steaming mug of coffee. As he
took a sip, his eyes landed on the notes he placed
earlier on the lounge table. Picking them up he
realized that he had no idea what to do with them. The
writing was unintelligible and some of the letters were
smudged. His thoughts drifted back to the curator,
Cecile Williams. She had been very friendly and
curious about the painting, too. She had never seen a
painting like it before and the painter's initials were
not familiar to her. Cecile checked her records and
there was no one with that artist signature or a record
of the painting. Steven had watched Cecile carefully
remove the backing of the frame. There had been
nothing strange or unusual about the frame, except
two small notes were found hidden behind the
painting. On one note were scribbles and smudged
writing, the other had a picture or a kind of drawing.
Cecile had told him that the painting was only about
four or five years old. It was not as old as what he had
originally thought. Fingering the notes he laid them
flat on the table to take a closer look and try decipher

the contents. An hour later, feeling drained, he gave up. Tomorrow would be another day.

Houlton Regional Hospital was buzzing with patients waiting, nurses running around, reception tending to all queries and admissions. Steven remained in his office. The door that bore his name *Dr. Steven Hudson, MD* engraved on a golden plaque was closed. There was a knock on the door. It was his colleague, Dr. Mike Hodgeson. He seemed slightly irritated and flustered.

"Hey, Steven ," Dr. Mike frowned. "What you doing? It's crazy out there."

"Sorry, Mike." Steven rubbed his temples, feeling a headache brewing. "I'm not myself today."

"I can see that. You look terrible." He sat on the chair opposite Steven . "What's that you holding?"

As much as Steven liked his colleague, he found Mike's curiosity annoying at times, then again, that is what made him an excellent Doctor.

Steven sighed. "I have no idea. I can't make anything of it."

"Let me take a look." Mike took the two notes from Steven and squinted while he concentrated on the notes. After a few minutes, he handed them back to Steven .

"You're right," His hands folded across his chest. "It's puzzling and looks childlike, but I think that drawing could be Wiley Pond. Yes, I really think so. In Patten, you know it?"

Steven shook his head.

"Before the baby came along, my wife and I, with a couple of friends, were always camping." Dr. Mike nodded. "I'm pretty sure that's Wiley Pond, because that square thing with those squiggles all around it, my guess, is a house, is Bradford Farm. It's now a bed and breakfast."

"In Patten?" Steven looked at the note of the drawing again. "It's a couple of miles away from here."

"I'm not going to ask why, but if you want to drive all that way I can give you a map. The off-roads are quite twisty, and if you don't know where you

going, you'll get lost."

"And, the writing?"

"I don't know." Dr. Mike shrugged. "You'll have

to figure that one out."

Chapter Two

The week dragged on and Steven had to pull in extra

shifts. Friday afternoon, after one last scheduled

surgery he would follow Dr. Mike's map and head off

to Patten. Every day Steven studied the grotesque

painting, and became mesmerized by the woman.

Looking into those captivating ocean blue eyes, he felt

pity, there seemed to be sadness in them. If she was

real, maybe he could help her. He was sure he could

help her. No, he was determined to help her.

Four hours later and a quick stop at Walmart, Steven managed to get onto the I-95 S without much traffic interference. The painting placed in the trunk alongside an overnight bag filled with a few clothing and other items. Patten was only an hour's drive from Houlton, so a quick pass in Island Falls to ME-159 W and finally route 11 to Patten. A small wooden signboard welcomed him to Patten. A beautiful town once known for its lumbar, fishing and farming, unfortunately as time went by things changed and brought about many abandoned farms and houses that remained with history.

Bradford House Bed and Breakfast Farm set on 17-acres of land, a memorial dated back from 1840 listed in the National Register of Historic Places, was a beautifully quaint place. Steven decided to grab a bite to eat at Flatlanders BBQ Smokehouse. Maybe someone would know about these notes, or the woman in the painting. Maybe there was some kind of legend or a hidden secret within this town.

The restaurant was in full swing. Waiters fervently maneuvered between wooden tables and chairs neatly scattered, surrounded by people laughing and chattering. Steven decided on BBQ Ribs and a beer. Most people were young and probably would not be much help. A tall, robust man, most likely in his mid-forties, stood behind the bar, laughing with a crowd surrounding the far end of the bar counter.

Steven decided it could be a bit of a wait for his meal so he stood and approached the man. The crowd grew silent when Steven produced the notes and image of the painting he had saved on his phone earlier. Jack's earlier jovial manner changed to an abrupt deep frown as he held the notes and stared at the image.

"That's a real disgusting painting. Why would you want that piece of junk?" He handed the notes back to Steven. "Sorry, can't help you."

"This, here, is Wiley Pond. I believe the letters on this note may mean something.

Maybe, an address. Do you know anyone that could make out these letters?"

Jack looked amused. "Boys, do you have any ideas?"

Everyone shook their heads, followed by, no's and nope's. Some took gulps of their drinks, averting Steven 's gaze; others looked at the impressive boating décor displayed on the walls.

"See? No one knows anything. Your meal is ready, that's your table, right?" Jack nodded toward Steven 's table. "You better grab it before somebody else does. Enjoy your stay in Patten. Careful you don't come into any trouble. We're a peaceful place and we like to keep it that way."

After thanking Jack and the group, Steven returned to the table and devoured his meal. There was no doubt that this was one of the best BBQ ribs he'd ever had and Jack's behavior disturbed him. The other men were not keen to look at the notes or the image of the painting. If it were nothing, why would Jack say what he did? Jack knew something. Steven felt it in his gut and a shiver ran down his spine. Was there a hidden secret behind this painting? Maybe the woman had lived here, and had been part of a diabolical agenda. Seeing, as no one would help him, tomorrow he would begin his hunt from Wiley Pond.

The overcast clouds promised signs of rain later. Steven made a mental note to visit the Lumbermens Museum if he had time as he drove past the building, driving the simple four-and-a-half-miles straight road from Patten to Wiley Pond. Steven gave a brief glace at the letter on the passenger seat. Someone slid an envelope with a simple letter underneath his hotel door during the night. The letter neatly typed, read, *"If you continue what you seek, you'll find demise"* on plain white paper. The only people in Patten that knew about the painting were Jack and his crowd of friends.

The road came to a split between Waters road and Frenchville Road, Steven continued straight onto a dusty dirt road that led to Wiley Pond. Steven remembered Dr. Mike telling him about the Pond, more of a lake than a pond, great for fishing and very isolated, quiet and peaceful. A few narrow dirt roads led beyond the trees into the forest. He looked at the notes again, and compared them with Dr. Mike's map. He interpreted the three squiggles to be some kind of pathway, one to the left of the pond, one going around the pond, and one to the right of pond. On Dr. Mike's map, there were more than three roads. Steven closed his eyes, held his breath and pointed at a random location on the map. The first try ended up somewhere south of Patten. He knew he was wasting time and decided to try the one on the right. The dirt road was very narrow and bumpy. A few drops of rain scattered across the windshield. Great, Steven thought. He had no idea how far this road was and no desire to be stuck in a muddy dirt road. He sped up the pace, carefully trying to avoid the deep rocky potholes. After what felt like hours, Steven came to a rundown, dilapidated looking cabin. How it was still standing was a mystery. As more drops began to fall,

Steven gathered his belongings as fast as he could and ran to the cabin. Steven found the door unlocked and entered. He placed his belongings on the floor and rubbed his arms. He was glad to have thought to bring the extra jacket. The cabin smelt musty, the floorboards creaked with his every step and the eerie silence was deafening.

"Hey, hey there?" The cabin answered with an echo, then silence. He called out again and moved forward, deeper into the cabin. He could hear the rain begin to grow louder, hitting hard against the wooden structure and wondered if the cabin would hold.

Other than what looked like a lounge and dining room with no furniture, and a kitchen with the bare necessities, there was nothing. He called out again and only the cabin answered him. It seemed this would be his lodging for the night. He climbed the staircase, careful to test each wooden step. He found three rooms, and what looked like a bathroom, there was an old dusty single bed in the first room, nothing in the second and as he approached the third room, sounded a meticulous creaking like a rocking noise. The door hinges whined as Steven slowly opened it and softly called out if anyone was there. The rocking stopped and Steven 's heart began to beat faster. Someone was there.

"Hello?" He stared at a figure dressed in black seated in a rocking chair, the back facing him, staring out the window. "I'm very sorry to intrude. The door was unlocked and the rain started to fall harder."

The figure started rocking in the chair again. As the clouds gathered, the cabin became darker. There were no light switches. Of course, he wanted to kick himself, as such an old cabin in the middle of nowhere would not have the luxury of electricity.

"It's getting dark. Do you have any lamps or some kind of lighting?" He sighed, when the person ignored him. "My name is Steven."

"Steven" The voice repeated in a soft whisper. "Go away."

"Um, actually, the weather is getting worse. Could I use the room with the bed?" There was no answer so Steven continued, "I could sleep downstairs,

otherwise my car-"

"I said, leave." The voice was suddenly abrupt. "Get

out!"

A crack of thunder and the cabin shuddered, the

floor vibrated, and Steven fell to the floor. "I guess,

the car it is, then." Steven whispered to himself.

He retraced his steps back downstairs to fetch his

belongings.

"Wait!" The woman's voice sounded at the top of

the staircase. "You can stay. One night only. Then

leave."

After thanking her, Steven settled in the first

room with the dusty bed. Although it was getting

darker in the cabin, it was still the afternoon, and he

forgot to bring food with him and his stomach

growled. He had not realized his trip would end up

like this and knew he would have to go speak to that

person again. Judging by the voice, it was a woman, a

young woman. Why would she want to stay in a place

like this?

Steven found her in the same room, seated on the rocking chair, and continued to stare out the window.

"I just want to thank you, again, for letting me stay, and, uh, what is your name?"

"Why are you here", she asked

"The rain, and…"

"No! Why did you come out here?"

Steven slowly began to tell her all the events from the time he found the painting. As his story became more vivid in his mind, he stepped closer to her.

"Stay back! Don't come any closer."

"And, now, all I want to do is…". His blood turned to ice as his voice trailed off, a sliver of light through the window brushed across her face,

"Is to find … you."

Chapter Three

Steven 's eyes widened as he stared at the person who lived within the frame of the painting right before his eyes. The actual person in her grotesque form lived here. Her sharp eyes blue as the ocean, stared at him, and her hair gold swirled around her mangled disfigured swollen face, covered with yellow mucus secreting from infected lesions. Her pale skin had red pimpled patches, with silvery flaky scales. She was not an old woman as he had suspected, but a young woman, possibly in her early twenties.

"How did you find me?" Her voice trembled.

"The painting," Steven pulled out his phone, found the image and showed it to her. "There were notes hidden behind the painting."

"Fine, you found me. Now leave."

"What happened to you? You're-"

"Did you just come here to gawk at me?!" She said angrily and turned to look at him. Steven could not help looking away. She truly was a monster.

"No, no, I came to help you. Isn't that what you wanted?" He handed her the notes. "I still can't decipher the writing, but the drawing led me here.

Only by sheer luck, I came across this cabin. You've got to believe me."

"I haven't seen these in a long time," She said, handing the notes back to Steven .

"It's names of the Doctors, and I think the Lab's location. How can *you* help me?"

"I'm a Doctor. Let me examine you and…"

"A Doctor?" She laughed bitterly. "Why should I trust you? You're an intruder."

Steven cleared his throat. "I want to help and find out what is wrong with you."

"What's wrong with me!? I'll tell you what"s wrong with me!" She looked away as tears began to slide down her swollen, red, flaky cheeks. "You Doctors are all the same. Use fancy words. Wear masks, poking with needles, inflicting pain, lots of pain. Look at me now! All for the good of *Science*."

"Please, trust me; give me a chance to help you."

"Did anyone follow you?"

"Uh, no, I don't think so." He shrugged, "Besides, I think the weather would put off anyone if they even thought to follow me."

After examining her, Steven realized that she did not have a form of leprosy, psoriasis, or any kind of disease. This was an abnormality that he'd never seen before, but treatable.

The rain began to subside and Steven promised to return the next day with medication for her skin, painkillers and anti-inflammatories, before he could perform any surgery.

"Emma" She said suddenly. "My name is Emma Lewis."

E.L. The initials at the bottom of the painting.

As promised Steven returned the next day, and again the next day, with the medication, antibiotics, bacterial cream to treat the lesions on Emma's face, and every time had to convince her it was safe to take the anti-inflammatory medication.

"Do you not remember anything more about the Doctors?" Steven asked as he gently inserted a needle just below the skin surface near her eyebrow. "I really wish you would come with me to the hospital. One of my colleagues could perform a light cosmetic procedure.”

“I remember them talking strange things, I didn’t understand.”

“They didn’t say what they were doing or why?”

Emma shook her head slowly. “They said things like DNA, genetic codes…ultimate human weapon.”

“The last I remember was one of the nurses, I think, she helped me escape.” Emma closed her eyes. “I think she brought me here. Told me to wait. Someone used to bring me food and other supplies, but it’s been some time since they have come.”

“Emma, I did some research at the hospital and it looks like a large corporation bought some land here a few years ago, between Pickett Mountain and Mount Chase. There is no other information. It’s all classified.”

“What does that mean?”

“I’m not sure.” Steven frowned, “It sounds suspicious and there have been rumors of a secret lab somewhere in Maine. By the way, who painted the painting of you?"

"I did." Emma sighed, "I remember being inside a white room with no windows.

I could barely make out where the door was, but I created my own room. The food they gave me was disgusting so I used the food to paint the white walls. I thought it was good. When the nurse brought me here, she left me with art supplies."

"How did the painting end up in Portland, then?"

"It doesn't happen often that people come out this way." Emma giggled. "After what the nurse said to me, I was scared of my own shadow. People would come and stay up this way, for usually a week or so. I had to hide my presence. I tried to make a basic frame for the painting, and I'm not a carpenter so it didn't come out really well. I scribbled those notes and hid them behind the canvas and put the painting in my basic frame and left it near one of the tents."

As Steven listened to Emma, he couldn't help but wonder if she was hiding something or if she really didn't remember, maybe she didn't want to remember.

The progress on Emma's face had been going well and Steven bought a mirror for her so she could see the results of every treatment and surgical procedure.

"I have a surprise for you, Emma. There is some cosmetic work to be done on your face and I have found a way that does not require plastic surgery." Her ocean blue eyes stared at him in surprise.

Blushing slightly, he looked away and added, "It's a Plasma device that makes the skin heal itself. Soon, you will be back to your beautiful self." Every time Steven visited Emma, he could not shake the feeling he was being watched. Perhaps it was because of the letter that had been slipped underneath his hotel door when he stayed at Bradford House. He kept the secret lab conspiracy theory to the back of his mind, putting it down as being paranoid. Just to be safe he kept the letter in his glove compartment. Since then, he had not received any kind of threatening notes and had no reason to worry. The only thing he became worried about was that he couldn't stop thinking about Emma. It was not appropriate to

develop feelings for a patient, but then again, she was
not really a patient. He wondered, hoped, if she felt
the same?

Chapter Four

Emma held up the emerald green dress that Steven
had bought her and smiled. Steven grew to love that
smile and was over the moon that she accepted to go
with him to the cinema. After the last few arduous
months, they both needed a break. She needed to be
treated and made to feel special. After one night at the
cinema, and a few trips to local restaurants, Emma
became more confident and went out with Steven
often. She smiled more and laughed.

"Stay with me forever", she said, holding his
hand as they sat near Wiley Pond sheltered by the
trees. It was quite late so Steven decided to stay over
again and lay beside her.

A sudden noise jolted Steven awake, his heart raced in anxiety. He heard something, a noise, as if someone had broken down the door. He shook Emma gently and whispered in her ear to stay still. Slowly he climbed out the bed and as quietly as possible, at each step he tried to prevent the floorboards from creaking under his weight. He thought if he could make it to the kitchen and find a carving knife he could ward off the burglar. As he grabbed the carving knife, he heard Emma scream. He whipped around and faced a figure wearing a black mask. Someone behind placed a cloth over his face, chloroform, and everything went black.

It was so dark, dark as a closet. Where was Emma? Steven woke up strapped on a cold stretcher. He looked down and saw he was dressed in a white gown. Hospital, secret lab, echoed through his mind. His body felt like fire. He looked around, he appeared to be in an operating room. He could feel his face was bandaged, and his arms and legs, and across his chest. Why was he covered in bandages? He had to get out of here. He had to find Emma. Struggling under the straps, he managed to get free. Without thinking he just ran. The passageways were empty and he managed to get out of the hospital. Where was everyone? He needed to get help and then find Emma. Steven 's body burned with pain, but he kept going. He recognized the terrain, the forest, and knew it would be a long stretch, but he would end up in Patten's main street if he kept going. Taking deep breaths, his lungs felt like they were burning.

After what felt like hours, he came to a small river, and just beyond that was the road to the Main Street. Bending down he drank from the river, he didn't realize how parched he was. Feeling slightly better, he continued to run following the stretch of the road. He looked back every so often and hoped no one was after him. Finally, he arrived at the Main Street and all the shops and restaurants were closed. He knew there was a gas station nearby, and in slow steady steps, made his way to find it. Driving was easy, on foot, was another thing. Steven tried to remember what happened, but all he remembered was

Emma's screams and then darkness. He had no idea
how he ended up in that hospital and why he was
strapped to the stretcher in an operating room. There
was no one around at the gas station and he found the
men's bathroom, it was not locked. He began to
remove the bandages from his arms and found
stitches, painful to the touch, the same on his legs and
his chest. Steven saw a small dirty mirror mounted
above a small sink. His face was covered in bandages.

Carefully he removed the bandages, and dread
filled his mind as he swirled the bandages from his
head. He stared at his distorted reflection, thinking it
was the mirror. Touching his face, realization hit him
as if burning coals had been dumped over his head.
His face looked like railway tracks covered in stitches,
patches of skin missing and stretched over parts of his
face. Some skin patches did not match his own. How
many other people had been victim to this patchwork
for so many different skin types to be stitched to his
face? And, for what reason?

He heard a car stop at the gas station and turned

to run out the bathroom, in hope the driver would help

him. A noise made him stop and he turned around.

The mirror fell down. Frowning he went to pick up the

mirror and froze with horror as he turned the mirror

over. It was not a mirror. It was a painting and he

stared at his own life-like disfigured portrait with the

background of a gas station.

***

Christian Stahl

Details of all the author's available books and upcoming titles

can be found at:

www.shortstoriesforbeginners.com